BACK IN SOCIETY

Driven into hiding at the hotel by a tyrannous father, Lady Jane Fremney attempts to end her life. The poor relations save the young lady and determine to improve her lot in life by bringing her out for the Season. All the young bucks call on Jane, among them the handsome but racy Comte de Mornay, an exile from Napoleon's France who has broken many a heart and so far eluded matrimony. Jane is quite adamant he is unsuitable for her – but when his life is threatened by an assassin's pistol, it is up to her to help him escape from danger ... and into *l'amour!*

BACK IN SOCIETY

BACK IN SOCIETY

by

M. C. Beaton

Magna Large Print Books
Long Preston, North Yorkshire,
BD23 4ND, England.

British Library Cataloguing in Publication Data.

Beaton, M. C.
    Back in society.

    A catalogue record of this book is
    available from the British Library

    ISBN   978-0-7505-4146-6

First published in Great Britain by Canvas,
an imprint of Constable & Robinson Ltd., 2013

Cover illustration by arrangement with
Little, Brown Book Company

Published in Large Print 2015 by arrangement with
Little, Brown Book Group

Magna Large Print is an imprint of Library Magna Books Ltd.

Printed and bound in Great Britain by
T.J. (International) Ltd., Cornwall, PL28 8RW

For Ann Robinson and her daughter,
Emma Wilson, with love.

ONE

The poor always ye have with you.
THE BIBLE

The Poor Relation was no longer an apt name for what had become London's most fashionable hotel. The Prince of Wales's coat of arms gleamed over the entrance with that magic legend 'By Special Appointment.' In residence and taking up every guest room except one for his retinue of friends and servants was Prince Hugo Panič, from some Middle European country which everyone swore they had heard of but no one seemed to know anything about.

The owners of the hotel had been poor relations themselves when they founded it, that despised shabby genteel class eking out a difficult living. But Lady Fortescue, Sir Philip Sommerville, Colonel Sandhurst, and Miss Tonks, the owners, had made it prosper, at first by theft from their relations, and then by a combination of guile, hard business and luck. An actor, Mr Jason Davy, had recently bought his way into shared ownership, and yet, because of old Sir Philip's jealousy and dislike of him, had never felt he was one of them.

The open-handed prince paid hard cash as he went along and the hoteliers felt their days of penury were truly behind them. This gave them an added happiness and sparkle, and even Sir Philip had not been heard to utter anything loathsome for quite a number of days.

But their very happiness intensified the black misery of the occupant of the one apartment not taken up by the prince or his entourage. The occupant was Lady Jane Fremney, youngest daughter of the Earl of Durby. Through her refusal to marry the man her father had picked out for her, she had been cast out 'until she came to her senses.' That, her father considered, would not take very long as she had only one small trunk of clothes and none of her jewellery.

Lady Jane had used what was left of her pin money to travel from Durbyshire to London. She thought back on her miserable, lonely childhood, thought of her bullying governess, thought of the family servants who had treated her harshly because her father, the earl, encouraged them to do so.

'You have to break a woman's spirit to make her a good wife' was one of his favourite maxims, and Lady Jane often wondered whether that was why her mother had gone to such an early grave, when she herself was but two years old.

So she decided to put an end to her life. She had told the owner of the Poor Relation that her maid would be arriving shortly. Her empty jewel case was weighted down with stones.

She ate by herself at a corner table in the dining room, only half interested in the noisy, garrulous prince who sat at the centre table with his equally noisy mistress. She picked at the delicious food which the hotel always served, hardly tasting what she ate. She did not notice the owners much, and a London hotel being such an anonymous sort of place, she supposed that they barely noticed her.

In this she was wrong.

Four days after her arrival, the owners were gathered in their private sitting room at the top of the hotel. They looked very different from the threadbare people who had first banded together to share their lot. Lady Fortescue, in her seventies, tall and erect, wore a cap of fine lace on top of her snowy, impeccably coiffured hair, and a silk gown of expensive cut. Colonel Sandhurst, very grand in Weston's best tailoring, and occasionally glancing down at the shine on his flat pumps, fiddled with a diamond stickpin in his cravat and beamed around at everyone with his mild, childlike blue eyes. Also in his seventies, his one ambition now was to sell the hotel and marry Lady Fortescue.

Sir Philip Sommerville, equally old, was quite the dandy in a padded coat and enormous cravat. His tortoise-like face looked unusually benign, but then Sir Philip claimed that money could make a saint out of anyone.

Miss Tonks, fortyish, or, as Lord Byron put it, a lady of certain years, years uncertain, had a certain elegance, not entirely due to French taffeta and the clever hands of the royal hairdresser. She no longer blinked nervously or hung her head. She was as erect and confident a figure now as Lady Fortescue, and her gentle, sheeplike face turned from time to time towards the door, awaiting the arrival of the man of her dreams, Mr Jason Davy.

Just when she was beginning to think he would never arrive, Mr Davy entered. He was a middle-aged man, slim and nondescript, with bright eyes and thick brown hair streaked with grey. He, like Colonel Sandhurst, was impeccably dressed, and the only person who thought that he never could, never would look like a gentleman was Sir Philip Sommerville. Sir Philip had marked down Miss Tonks to take care of him in his declining years, but the 'silly' spinster did nothing but make sheep's eyes at the actor.

And Miss Tonks then proceeded to dent Sir Philip's new-found euphoria by saying eagerly, 'I am so glad you are come, Mr Davy. We have a problem.'

Mr Davy smiled and sat down next to her. 'What problem?' demanded Sir Philip with a scowl.

'Why, Lady Jane, to be sure,' said Miss Tonks.

'Oh, that one. I am sure she hasn't a feather to fly with, and what's more, doesn't mean to pay her bill.' Sir Philip tapped his nose. 'I can smell poverty. But does it matter? We're in funds. She's a beautiful lady, so we may as well be charitable for a change. She's in the poorest rooms. She can stay for a month and we'll give her a bill and if she don't pay it, we'll kick her out.'

'That is no answer to the problem,' said Lady Fortescue. 'I, too, have remarked on

Lady Jane's downcast looks. She is the daughter of the Earl of Durby and yet no one calls on her, nor does she call on anyone. The maid she spoke of has not arrived. She seems to walk and move in misery.'

'Do you mean she might commit suicide?' asked Mr Davy.

'Here now!' Sir Philip sat up straight, his pale eyes registering alarm. 'That would be a disaster. Get a suicide and the place is damned. Our prince would take himself off and it would be ages before anyone else would come. But what has she to commit suicide about? She may be poor and obviously in trouble with her family, but she is beautiful.'

'Perhaps she does not know it,' said Colonel Sandhurst. 'What lady so sunk in misery as she obviously is can think of her looks? How old is she, would you say?'

'Nineteen or twenty,' said Lady Fortescue. 'Her father is a brute, I believe, her mother dead, her four brothers in the military.'

'Let's get back to this suicide business.' Sir Philip was becoming increasingly worried. 'I mean, how do we stop her?'

'Perhaps,' volunteered Mr Davy, 'she might confide in one of us.'

'Meaning you?' jeered Sir Philip. 'Always

the ladies' man, hey.'

'I was thinking of Miss Tonks here,' said Mr Davy, casting a forgiving smile on Sir Philip, which irritated that elderly gentleman every bit as much as Mr Davy had meant it to do.

'I have tried twice to engage her in conversation,' said Miss Tonks, 'but she looks at me with such blank eyes that I cannot go on. But I will try to watch her as closely as I can.

'You can't be with her every minute of the day and night,' pointed out Colonel Sandhurst. 'Would not the best course of action be to write to her father? He cannot know she is alone and unchaperoned in London.'

'Let us see what Miss Tonks can find out,' said Lady Fortescue. 'We have had enough trouble in the past. It is time to enjoy comfort and to look after ourselves. Someone as young and as beautiful as Lady Jane may be distressed for the moment, but suicide! No, I think not.'

Miss Tonks slept late the following day. She had recently become accustomed to that luxury because the hotel had now a highly paid, efficient staff. It was well known among the servant class that the Poor Relation paid for the best and would sack anyone who was not willing, bright and efficient.

But her first uneasy thought was about Lady Jane. She washed and dressed hurriedly in her room in the apartment which the hoteliers rented. It was next door to the hotel.

When she entered the entrance hall, a heavily veiled figure walked past her and out into Bond Street. Sure that it was Lady Jane, Miss Tonks turned about and followed in pursuit.

Ragged clouds raced over the dingy sky above. Miss Tonks hoped it would not rain, for rain turned the streets of London into slippery, muddy hazards, and she was not wearing pattens, those wooden clogs with the high iron ring on the sole, so useful in wet weather. A strong wind was howling down the narrow streets and sending streams of smoke snaking down from the whirling cowls on the chimney-pots. Ahead of her, the slim figure of Lady Jane moved easily and quickly, heading always in the direction of the City. By the time Miss Tonks and her quarry reached the bottom of Ludgate Hill, Miss Tonks was feeling tired. Up the hill went Lady Jane and then turned off into one of the narrow lanes where the apothecaries had their shops. Miss Tonks saw her go into one of these shops and hesitated outside, peering in over the display of leeches in jars and coloured bottles of liquid. She saw Lady Jane buy two flat green bottles of something. She drew back into a doorway as Lady Jane emerged, and then, as she watched her hurrying off, Miss Tonks wondered what to do. After a little hesitation, she pushed open the door of the apothecary's and went in.

'I wonder,' said Miss Tonks to the assistant, 'whether my lady's-maid has just been here. I sent her to buy something for me, but as I was in the City, I thought I would find out, you see, whether she had bought it. A heavily veiled woman.'

'I have just sold two bottles of laudanum to a veiled lady,' said the assistant.

'Oh, really? Yes, that is it. I have great difficulty sleeping at night.' And Miss Tonks chattered her way out of the door, discoursing all the while on her mythical sleeplessness.

On Ludgate Hill, she hailed a hack to take her back to Bond Street, where she called her partners together and told them of Lady Jane's purchase.

'A lot of ladies take laudanum,' said Mr Davy.

'Fool!' said Sir Philip. 'Not two whole bottles of the stuff. I have it. We'll get Jack, the footman, to collect her as soon as she has deposited the stuff in her room. I'll take her into the office and say that bills should be settled monthly, a new policy, and we will be presenting her with her account at the end of the month. I will hold her in conversation. Perhaps then Lady Fortescue and Miss Tonks can go to her room and change the mixture for something innocuous.'

'But why not confront her with the fact that we suspect she plans to do away with herself?' said the colonel.

'All she has to do is lie,' said Sir Philip. 'She'll leave a note for her father. Bound to. I know, leave enough laudanum in the bottles to knock her out. We'll keep checking on her and as soon as we find she's left a note, then we'll have her and out she goes.'

'Oh, no, we cannot do that,' exclaimed Miss Tonks. 'It would only add to her shame and wretchedness. Yes, we find her out and then we try to do something to help!'

Sir Philip groaned and clutched at his wig so that it slipped sideways. 'Look, we're happy and rich and we've got our generous prince to thank for it. Why bother ourselves with some mad girl?'

'Because it is our duty,' said Lady Fortescue awfully, and that silenced Sir Philip.

Lady Jane walked along Bond Street. Rain was beginning to fall, an appropriate day to end her life. She could feel the dragging weight of the two bottles of laudanum in her reticule. She had found her way to Ludgate Hill because one of the maids had drawn her a map. She would write a letter to her father and beg him to settle her account at the hotel. A smart carriage moved past. A pretty girl looked out of the window. Two soldiers on the pavement stared at her boldly. Three young matrons followed by their footmen and lady's-maids sailed into the hotel, no doubt to take coffee, because the Poor Relation was really the only place in London outside of Gunter's, the confectioner's, where ladies could meet.

In her rooms, Lady Jane unpinned her hat and veil and threw them on a chair. She put the two bottles on the toilet-table and then crossed to the writing-desk in her small sitting room. She was just sharpening a quill with a penknife when there came a scratching at the door and Jack, the footman, walked in.

'My lady,' he said, 'Sir Philip Sommerville

requests the honour of your presence in the office.'

Lady Jane stood up. 'Where is this office?'

'At the back of the entrance hall, my lady.'

'Very well, I will follow you shortly.'

Jack hesitated on the threshold, remembering his instructions, which were not to leave her alone for a moment. 'I beg pardon, my lady, but Sir Philip said the matter was pressing.'

Lady Jane gave a little sigh. They had probably guessed that she had no maid following on. They would have noticed that no one called on her. They would be anxious to find out whether she could meet her bill or not. Well, it didn't matter any more. All she had to do was tell more lies.

'I will come with you,' she said.

Colonel Sandhurst and Mr Davy were also in the small office. They stood up as Lady Jane entered.

She was wearing a plain grey gown of some shimmering stuff which seemed to highlight her extreme pallor. She was, despite the shadows under her eyes and the look of strain on her face, still very beautiful. Her skin was without blemish and her eyes, very large and grey, were fringed with thick lashes. Her mouth was perfect.

'Do sit down, my lady,' urged Sir Philip. 'May we offer you some tea, or wine? Perhaps a glass of negus or ratafia?'

'Nothing, I thank you.' She sat down with an unconscious grace. 'I believe you have business to discuss with me. What is it?'

'We have a new policy in this hotel,' said Sir Philip, speaking very slowly and hoping Lady Fortescue and Miss Tonks were fast about their work. 'We expect bills to be settled at the end of each month. I hope this does not disturb you.'

'Not at all,' said Lady Jane with the fleeting shadow of a smile. 'Is there anything else?' She began to rise.

'Yes, yes,' said the colonel hurriedly. 'We hope you will not consider this an impertinence, my lady, but because of your extreme youth and because you are unchaperoned, we are naturally concerned for you.'

Her voice was quiet and even.

'I do consider it an impertinence.'

Mr Davy spoke for the first time. His voice was kind. 'Do not be angry with us. We have noticed your sad looks. When one feels most alone, one should always remember that there is someone to help.'

Lady Jane's eyes were lit with a flash of anger. Why couldn't they leave her alone? She was angriest at Mr Davy for his kindness, for arousing that anger in her, for she preferred to stay wrapped in dull numb misery which would make what she had to do the easier.

She rose to her feet. Making an obvious effort, she said, 'I thank you for your concern, but it is not necessary, I assure you. Good day, gentlemen.'

'And that's that,' said Sir Philip gloomily. 'I hope she doesn't run into Lady Fortescue and Miss Tonks in her rooms.'

Lady Jane actually met both of them in the corridor outside. Lady Fortescue and Miss Tonks smiled and curtsied. She bowed her head and scurried past them and into her rooms. She locked the door behind her and then went to the writing-table. She sharpened the quill with swift, efficient strokes and drew sheets of writing-paper towards her. Should she blame her father for what she was about to do? No, she could not leave him with that misery. Perhaps he thought he had been doing only what was best for her. When she had turned out of her home, she had told him defiantly that she was going to stay with her old nurse in Yorkshire. The nurse, Nancy Thistlethwaite, had been the only person in her short life who had ever been kind to her and who had been fired as a result. Her father had laughed at her and had said that a poor existence in a cottage with that fool Nancy was just what was needed to bring her to her senses and agree to the marriage he had arranged for her.

So she wrote a letter saying simply that she had taken her own life and that she would like him to settle her hotel bill. Then she wrote another letter to Sir Philip Sommerville, apologizing for having committed suicide in the hotel and assuring him that her father would settle her bill. She sanded and sealed both letters and propped them up on the writing-table.

Then she brushed down her hair and took off her clothes and put on her nightgown. She poured the contents of both bottles into two glasses and, pinching her nose, swallowed down the contents, one glassful after the other.

She lay down carefully on top of the bed and sent a prayer up for forgiveness. She could feel herself becoming sleepy, and suddenly she began to fight against it. Out of nowhere came an intense desire to live. She dragged herself from the bed onto the floor. But a wave of misery hit her again and the desire to sleep was so very great. She would close her eyes just for a moment...

25

Jack, the footman, pressed his ear hard against the panel of the door. He thought he had heard a faint crash but Lady Jane's sitting room was on the other side of the door, not her bedchamber. He listened and listened but the following silence was absolute.

'Anything?' whispered Sir Philip behind him, making him jump.

'Nothing.'

'Then scratch the door and go in, man. Use your wits. Say it's a cold day and you wondered whether she would like the fires lit.'

Jack scratched at the panels and then turned the handle. 'It's locked!'

'Run and get the spare key out of the office, demme, and get the ladies up here.'

He fretted and chewed his knuckles in impatience. Jack returned, after what seemed to Sir Philip like an age, with not only the ladies but Colonel Sandhurst and Mr Davy as well. 'Now open the door,' whispered Sir Philip. 'You go in, Jack, and if all is well, ask her about the fires. If she's dead, call us.'

'She can't be dead,' said Lady Fortescue crossly. 'We emptied out most of the contents of the bottles and replaced them with plain water.

Jack unlocked the door and went in, very nervously. He hoped she would be in the sitting room, for if she was not, that meant she would be in the bedroom and might have locked the door to her room for no more sinister reason than because she wanted to change her clothes.

But the sitting room was empty. With a dry mouth he approached the open bedroom door and peered around it. No one. He gave a little sigh of relief and was about to turn away when he noticed one small bare foot sticking out from the floor on the far side of the bed. He walked round the bed and stared down at the still form of Lady Jane Fremney.

He rushed back through the sitting room, babbling, 'She's gone and done it. Oh, she's gone and done it.'

The others came in and crowded into the bedroom. Miss Tonks knelt down and bent over the girl. 'She is sleeping peacefully. God be thanked.'

Sir Philip retreated to the sitting room, where he found the two letters. He opened the one addressed to the hotel and let out a crow of triumph. 'We've got her!' he cried. He scuttled into the bedroom, waving the letter. 'And there's one addressed to her father.'

'Poor child,' murmured Lady Fortescue. 'Lift her onto the bed, Jack, and cover her with the quilt. Miss Tonks and I will be here when she awakes.'

Lady Jane slowly came awake. Her mind was immediately flooded with the realization of what she had done, of what she had tried to do. She was torn between misery that she was alive with her problems and relief that she was still alive. She struggled up against the pillows and her dazed eyes looked into those of Lady Fortescue and Miss Tonks, who were sitting beside the bed.

'What are you doing here?' she asked faintly.

Lady Fortescue ignored her. 'Tell Jack to bring the others here,' she ordered Miss Tonks.

'I must get up,' said Lady Jane feebly. She had just remembered the letters on the writing-desk.

Lady Fortescue held up one thin hand. 'In a moment. We know about the letters.'

Miss Tonks returned, followed by the colonel, Sir Philip and Mr Davy.

Lady Jane stared at them defiantly. She was beginning to remember falling on the floor. Someone had lifted her onto the bed and covered her.

'Now we are all here,' said Lady Fortescue, 'we would like to know how you came to take your own life.'

'A demned selfish action, too,' growled Sir Philip. 'Did you never think of us? A suicide could ruin us.'

'Do you mean the money for these rooms is all-important to you?' asked Lady Jane.

'Not the money – the scandal, the superstition. The next thing people would be seeing your ghost. Did it never dawn on you that your poor family would have to see you interred at the crossroads, with a stake through your heart?' complained Sir Philip, describing how suicides of the early-nineteenth century were buried.

'And did you not think of your immortal soul?' chided the colonel gently. 'What you planned on doing was a sin against God.'

'I know, I know,' said Lady Jane wretchedly. 'But what else could I do?'

'You could tell us how we may help you.' Miss Tonks pressed Lady Jane's hand. 'We are concerned for your plight.'

Lady Jane looked at the circle of faces around the bed.

'Very well, I will tell you. I had a most unhappy childhood. My problems really began when my father engaged a governess, a Miss Stamp, to educate me. Miss Stamp delighted in tormenting me and bullying me. When I appealed to my father, he told her about my complaint and suggested she beat me the harder because I was becoming wilful and spoilt. But I endured – how I endured! – for one day I knew her services would no longer be required and I would make my come-out and at least I would have a brief time when I could meet girls of my own age. But Miss Stamp was raised to the rank of companion and still had the schooling of me in etiquette and conversation. Still, there was hope of marriage to perhaps a kind man who would free me from bondage. I was allowed to attend balls at neighbouring houses, but always with Miss Stamp. I danced with some agreeable men, but when they came to call I was never allowed to entertain them.

'The final blow came when my father summoned me to his study and told me there would be no need to take me to London for a Season, for he had found a husband for me. This man he had chosen for me was Sir Guy Parrish, his friend, a man in his fifties, small and wizened, a five-bottle-a-day man. I said I would not marry him. I said I had lasted, had endured the tyranny of Miss

Stamp, had endured his tyranny because one day, I thought, I would at least have a Season and a chance to find a man of my choice. He ordered me from the house, only allowing me to take one trunk. I took my jewel box, which had been emptied, and weighted it down with stones, for I knew what I meant to do. I would die in the London that had been forbidden to me. But I told him that I was going to stay with my old nurse in Yorkshire. He laughed and said a spell of poverty – for he knew Nancy, my old nurse, to be poor – was just what I needed to bring me to my senses. And so I came to you. I am so very sorry.' She turned her head away and tears rolled down her cheeks.

Sir Philip often admitted to himself that he was given to over-sentimentality. He surprised the others by saying in a rallying voice, 'Here, now. We are here to look after you. All you need, dear lady, is a little *fun*. I am the first to admit you have the dreariest apartment in the hotel and you should not be alone here. Not fitting. You can move in with Miss Tonks in our apartment next door.'

'Yes, do,' said Miss Tonks. 'We can have chats and look at the shops together.'

'Too kind,' said Lady Jane faintly, 'but I have no claim on you. You do not owe me anything. On the contrary...'

'It would amuse us,' said Lady Fortescue. 'I know that people of our rank are not allowed to talk about money, but we, being in trade, feel free to discuss our funds as much as we please. And we are in funds, thanks to the munificence of Prince Hugo. I think we should order some gowns for you. Gowns are very important in times of distress. We shall leave you to dress and pack. Miss Tonks will return in an hour to conduct you to your new quarters.'

The hoteliers left her and went down to the office for a council of war.

'She won't try it again, will she?' asked Sir Philip anxiously.

'I do not think so,' said Lady Fortescue. 'You are to be praised, Sir Philip, for the generosity of your nature.' She smiled at him, her black eyes almost flirtatious, and the colonel scowled. Sir Philip smiled back and then kissed her hand, remembering that not so long ago he had rather fancied Lady Fortescue.

'It is a pity that she cannot have a Season.' Miss Tonks looked wistful. 'She is so very beautiful, she could be all the rage.'

'She cannot.' Lady Fortescue looked around the small group. 'We are now pretty much socially acceptable again, although we are in trade. I am invited to several small functions, as is Colonel Sandhurst. But that is not the same. Besides, even if we could bring her out, her father would read her name in the social columns and post south to take her home. He may yet come looking for her. She is supposed to be with that nurse in Yorkshire, is she not? Then I suggest we give her some money to send to her old nurse and letters to post to her father, harsh letters which will keep him at bay for a little. If she learns how to enjoy herself – it will strengthen her character. Too much adversity, as we know, is very weakening.'

'She need not use her own name,' suggested Miss Tonks hopefully. 'No one knows she is in London.'

'We can't call her Lady Anything Else,' jeered Sir Philip. 'The peerage would soon come alive to the fact they had an impostor in their midst.'

'She doesn't need to be titled. Something like Miss Jane North, heiress,' said Miss Tonks.

Lady Fortescue smiled at the middle-aged spinster indulgently. 'You are a matchmaker, Miss Tonks. You have dreams of finding her an eligible gentleman before her father finds *her*. But how could she be presented in society? Another ball here? We cannot while our prince is in residence.'

'What about Harriet?' asked Miss Tonks, looking eagerly around.

'The Duchess of Rowcester!' exclaimed Sir Philip. Harriet had been their cook when they first started the hotel. She had been a poor relation like the rest of them. Then the Duke of Rowcester had married her. She wrote to them all from time to time.

'Even if we should consider entertaining such a far-fetched idea,' said Lady Fortescue gently, 'you forget Harriet lost her child nearly a year ago.'

There was a sad little silence. Harriet's beloved baby daughter had been carried off in a typhoid epidemic.

'But don't you see,' said Miss Tonks stubbornly, 'helping Lady Jane would brighten her up. Give her an interest.'

'Her husband is her interest,' said Sir Philip, beginning to chew his knuckles, a sign he was worried. The others did not know that the necessary funds to start the hotel had been supplied by Sir Philip from a necklace he had stolen from the Duke of Rowcester before he married Harriet. He had substituted a clever fake. He knew the real necklace had not been sold, for he had been paying the jeweller from time to time to keep it intact until such time as he might have enough to reclaim it. But of late he had forgotten to make the payments. He did not want to have anything to do with the formidable duke again.

'But the duke is abroad in Italy. Some elderly relative's funeral,' protested Miss Tonks. 'I read that in the newspapers. We could write to dear Harriet. She has only to refuse. I mean, we are not constraining her to come.'

'What ridiculous fustian,' snapped Sir Philip. 'What rubbish. The girl's lucky to be alive. Oh, amuse yourself for a little by taking her about and buying her gowns. But we have no need to become involved in plots and plans and schemes any more.'

'I would like to see Harriet again,' said the colonel. 'You could write, Miss Tonks, and send her our love and explain Lady Jane's situation.'

'I forbid it!' shouted Sir Philip, startling them all.

Had he not been so vehement in his protest, the others might, on sober reflection, have dropped the idea.

But Mr Davy said in a chiding voice, 'I

35

really think what you want or do not want does not enter into the matter, Sir Philip. If Miss Tonks wishes to write to the Duchess of Rowcester, then that is her decision.'

This incensed Sir Philip the more. 'Miss Letitia Tonks used to be a quiet and respectable female before you came here with your nasty actor ways,' he said. 'You're always filling her mind with trash.'

'Please don't,' whispered Miss Tonks and began to cry.

'Now look what you've done,' raged the colonel.

'A pox on the lot of you,' howled Sir Philip and slammed out of the room.

'Do not cry,' said Mr Davy, putting an arm around Miss Tonks's shaking shoulders. 'You do what you think best.'

And the feel of that comforting arm sent Miss Tonks straight from the depths of misery to heaven.

TWO

I regard you with an indifference closely bordering on aversion.

ROBERT LOUIS STEVENSON

Harriet, Duchess of Rowcester, walked slowly along the terrace and thought of her husband. Things had been uneasy between them since the death of Emily, their beloved daughter. A peacock on the lawn in front of her let out a harsh scream and turned its moulting feathers to the sun.

She reflected that she had been glad to see him leave for Italy, for she could no longer feel affectionate towards him and shrank from his embrace. He had said that he would keep to his own bedchamber until she was fully recovered from the death of their child. Guilt and concern for him made her feel like a bad wife, and yet she could not bring herself to approach him, to heal the ever-widening breach she sensed between them.

She heard the post-boy's horn and wondered whether the duke had written to her from Dover, although he had said he would write when he reached Milan, his destination. But she hurried through the house, hoping all the same that he might have written, that he might have forgiven her. She stopped short in the middle of the Yellow Saloon as the awful thought struck her that he might never forgive her. She shook her head as if to dismiss it, but it obstinately would not go away. She had known for the past few months that his kindness and consideration towards her were slowly fading, to be replaced by resentment.

Sadly she walked on, through the chain of rooms, and so into the hall. The butler was arranging a small pile of letters on a silver tray.

'I will take them now,' said Harriet. She picked up the letters and retreated to the small morning room, which she had made her own. She put aside the ones addressed to her husband. There were three for herself. One was a bill from a London dressmaker, one a mercer's bill for a bolt of figured silk, and the third was from Letitia Tonks.

She opened Miss Tonks's letter, which was crossed and recrossed and difficult to read, Miss Tonks having written first across the paper and then diagonally one way and then the other. It started with news of how well they were doing since the prince had arrived, and then there was a long piece about how delightful a companion Mr Davy was and what an asset to the hotel. I wonder what happened there, thought Harriet, pausing in her reading and remembering an effusive letter a while ago in which a rapturous Miss Tonks had claimed that Sir Philip Sommerville was about to propose marriage to her. She tilted the page and started on the crossed writing. It took her some time to work out that it was a description of the attempted suicide of a certain Lady Jane Fremney, daughter of the Earl of Durby. Harriet read on through the long description of Lady Jane's running away from home, her penury, her desire for a Season, Miss Tonks's grand idea that if the young woman assumed another name and if someone like dear Harriet felt like opening up her town house and bringing Lady Jane out, then perhaps the dear girl might find herself a suitable husband instead of 'that monster' her father had chosen for her.

Harriet read the letter carefully to the end. She remembered her days at the Poor Relation with affection, the scares, the excitement, the warmth and the friendship, and gave a little sigh. To anyone else, Miss Tonks's suggestion would seem absolutely mad, but to Harriet, remembering her friends with affection, it was just the sort of idea they would dream up.

Why not? she thought suddenly. Why not find something unusual like this to occupy her mind instead of sitting and grieving for her lost child, and feeling guilty about her estranged husband?

She went to her writing-desk and penned a letter to Miss Tonks saying that she would be in London in two weeks' time and that they would discuss the matter then. Harriet did not want to give a definite yes until she had seen this Lady Jane. Anyone who did something so terrible, so drastic as trying to commit suicide might be mentally unbalanced.

Miss Jane North, as she was now called, submitted dutifully to the outings arranged for her by Miss Tonks and Mr Davy, who appeared to have been appointed her guardians. She tried hard to return their kindness by appearing cheerful, but she seemed to carry a greyness around with her, a remoteness. They promenaded around the shops, drove in the parks, took tea at Gunter's in Berkeley Square and went to the playhouse, where Mr Davy escorted them backstage and introduced them to the actors. Jane, who had never known any such freedom, could not yet appreciate any of it. She went everywhere heavily veiled, her eyes cast down, speaking in a low voice and only when spoken to.

Miss Tonks began to feel at her wits' end. Mr Davy said soothingly that it would take time. Someone who had so recently been in such despair as to want to commit suicide did not recover overnight. Jane had dutifully written to her old nurse, enclosing money and two letters for her father, one to be posted on immediately, the other in two weeks' time. But she did this on instruction, as she did everything else they told her to do.

And then the Duchess of Rowcester's letter arrived and Miss Tonks took it first to Lady Fortescue.

'Our cautious Harriet,' said Lady Fortescue, after she had read it carefully. 'And quite right to be cautious, too. She may decide against bringing out a young female who always looks as if she is about to attend her own funeral. The sad fact is that I find Lady Jane something of a bore.'

'Oh, no!' exclaimed Miss Tonks, clasping her thin hands together. 'She is always sad, but so *good* and so very beautiful.'

'You have always had a weakness for beauty,' said Lady Fortescue sympathetically. 'But there is nothing in her at the moment to attract any man. Even when she ate in the dining room, she failed to catch the eye of our most susceptible prince. Just in case Jane North, as we now must call her, has any hope left in her, we should not tell her about Harriet until Harriet has seen her and made up her mind what to do. Harriet may very well decide it is not worth the effort. The weather has been dreadful of late. If this incessant rain ever ceases, Jane might come about. Having to go abroad wearing calash and pattens is very lowering. Sensible dress does have a lowering effect on the spirits.

'Normally I would suggest putting her to work in the hotel, although we now do little work ourselves. Work might give her an interest. On the other hand, should Harriet decide to sponsor her, then having been seen about the hotel working would ruin her social chances. Then, of course, for it actually to work out, Jane has to be lucky enough to find a suitor able to stand up to her father, and one rich enough not to care if he decides not to give her a dowry. Where are you taking her on this awful day?'

42

'We are going to the Park in a closed carriage.'

'The day is depressing enough without being confined in a closed carriage and looking out at a lot of muddy trees. I think perhaps Sir Philip should take her in hand.'

Miss Tonks primmed her lips in disapproval. 'Sir Philip is enough to drive anyone to suicide.'

'He can be waspish and irritating. But perhaps the girl has been treated to *too* much kindness and understanding.'

Miss Tonks was about to protest, but then she thought that a day without Jane would mean she could go to the Park with Mr Davy alone. 'I do not know how Sir Philip will entertain her,' she said instead. 'He will probably take her to a cock-fight.'

Sir Philip received Lady Fortescue's suggestion without enthusiasm. 'I don't know where to take her,' he grumbled. 'Why should I waste time escorting a Friday-faced antidote? And she goes about so heavily veiled, it's like speaking to one of those horrors out of a Gothic romance. Oh, well, I can see from that militant look in your eye that there is no escape. And talking about Friday-faced antidotes, where is our Miss Tonks?'

'I think she is going out with Mr Davy.'

'Meaning you know she is going out with Mr Davy, as usual. She is wasting her time on that mountebank and becoming skittish and frivolous, which is disgusting in a lady of her years.'

'Then,' said Lady Fortescue drily, 'it follows that you are even more disgusting when you are skittish and frivolous because you are nearly twice her age. With any luck, at the end of the next Season, we will all be able to sell up and retire. You seem to harbour some odd notion of marriage to Miss Tonks. It would not serve.'

'Why?'

'I shall put it crudely and bluntly. Miss Tonks is a genteel virgin and you are an old rip with carnal lusts which seem to increase with age. One would have thought lust would have turned to rust by now.'

'We should all stay together,' said Sir Philip sulkily. 'Davy's an interloper.'

'Mr Davy is one of us. He has proved his worth by being a most efficient debt collector. We have not one outstanding debt now. And now that the prince is here and his secretary is paying everything at the end of each week, we have no worries on that score. Mr Davy has earned a holiday, as have we all.'

'He was not with us from the beginning,' protested Sir Philip. 'He has had an easy time of it.'

'I am not going to waste any more time talking to you.' Lady Fortescue rose to her feet. 'Do what you can for Jane. You are a kind man at heart, Sir Philip, so stop trying to pretend otherwise.'

Sir Philip found Jane in the room she shared with Miss Tonks. She was wearing a carriage dress and the inevitable depressing hat with a heavy veil.

'I'm taking you out, see?' said Sir Philip, 'So I'll wait for you in the hotel office next door while you change.'

'Change?' asked the voice softly from behind the veil.

'Yes, change. You're going out with a fashionable gentleman, so put on something pretty and leave off that demned veil!'

Sir Philip walked out before she could reply.

Jane rose stiffly – she always moved stiffly these days, as if the mental pain inside her head had affected her movements – a rheumatism of the very soul – and went to the large carved press next to the fireplace and opened it. There were four new gowns which had arrived from the dressmaker's, neatly folded. On the top shelf were new hat-boxes. Although she had stood patiently while she was fitted for her new clothes, she had not worn any of them.

She selected a morning gown of white lace and muslin and a pelisse of apricot silk lined with fur. On her head she put an apricot velvet hat with a low crown and wide brim. She studied herself in the long mirror, not really seeing herself, not noticing the fashion plate that looked back at her, searching only for bits of loose thread or hair that might be caught in her clothes.

Sir Philip, when he saw her entering the office, surveyed her with delight. 'Now you look more the thing,' he crowed. 'And bless us all, but the sun has begun to shine.'

'Has it?' asked Jane. 'I did not notice.'

He clicked his tongue in impatience. 'I have ordered an open carriage. I tried to persuade the others that it was time we had our own carriage instead of running up an enormous bill at the livery stables. But would they listen? Not them. Cheese-paring when they don't have to be, and profligate when times are hard. Come.' He held out his arm and she dutifully placed her gloved hand on it. Sir Philip led her out into the hallway just as

Prince Hugo was arriving. Prince Hugo was a large, ebullient man with bushy side-whiskers and Slav eyes, intense blue eyes of an almost oriental cast. Those eyes fell on Jane and widened slightly. The prince's hand went up to his whiskers and gave them a twirl.

'Present me, Sommerville,' he said.

'Miss Jane North, Your Highness,' said Sir Philip.

The prince kissed Jane's gloved hand. She curtsied low. Sir Philip held out his arm again and they left the hotel while the prince stared after them.

'Made a conquest there,' said Sir Philip cheerfully as Jack helped them both into the carriage. 'Drive us around where we can be seen,' he instructed the coachman.

Jane sat rigidly beside him, missing the protection of her veil. So many people seemed to stop on the pavements to stare at her. She wondered if she had a smut on her nose.

She had never been told she was beautiful. It had been dinned into her mind from an early age that she was plain, and any hopes she had of attracting a man must be supplied by her rank and her dowry. At last the stares became too much.

'Sir Philip,' she said to that elderly gentleman, who was sitting with his arms folded, looking all about him with a complacent air. 'Why do people stare so? Do I have a mark on my face?'

'Pay them no heed and worry only when they stop staring. They like staring at beauties.'

He glanced at her astonished face and gave a cackle of laughter. 'No wonder you didn't know you were beautiful, moping around behind a veil and wishing you were dead because of some nasty old tyrant of a father.'

A faint flush rose up in her pale face. Had either Miss Tonks or Mr Davy told her she was beautiful, she would not have believed them, would have thought they were being kind. But Sir Philip's blunt remarks had the ring of truth. She looked about her with a sort of wonder. A tall guardsman stopped short on the pavement and looked at her in open admiration and raised his hat. Jane gave a polite bow.

'Here now,' admonished Sir Philip. 'If you haven't been introduced to 'em, you don't notice 'em. Where will I take you to blow the cobwebs out of your brain? We'll go down to the river.'

He called to the coachman to take them to Westminster Bridge, and when they reached there ordered Jane to dismount and told the driver to wait.

They walked along the bridge and into one of the semi-circular bays which overlooked the river. London lay covered in a misty haze through which a warm sun shone, turning everything to gold. Upstream lay the terraces of trees and grey houses in front of Westminster Hall, the new Millbank Penitentiary, and low banks lined with willow trees. Downstream were the ramshackle taverns and the warehouses of Scotland Yard, the gardens of Northumberland House, the conical watertower of York Buildings, Somerset House rising above the water, and St Paul's dome, dominating all the houses and spires. They stood in silence. The great stream flowed below them, green and grey, boats with white and brown sails scudding across it.

'It's beautiful,' said Jane.

'Nice enough on a good day,' said Sir Philip. 'I know, we'll go to the tea-gardens at Chelsea and enjoy the sunshine.'

The King's Road in Chelsea was a depressing sight with wounded soldiers standing outside the taverns, leaning on their crutches, their eyes wild with drink. But once Sir Philip and Jane were ensconced in the quiet of the tea-gardens, war seemed very far away, and

Napoleon a forgotten ogre.

'Thank you. This is very pleasant,' said Jane. 'I am indebted to you, as I am to your friends.'

'Then you can repay us by stopping feeling so disgustingly sorry for yourself,' said Sir Philip.

She stared at him, shocked, and then said coldly, 'Perhaps we should be getting back.'

'Not till I've said my piece.' Sir Philip tapped his cup with his spoon. 'You have had a hard time of it, no doubt about that, but society is full of folk who were whipped by their parents, shut up in the cellar, and, yes, girls who were forced into marriage with men they don't like. It's the way of the world. But you lack bottom. If the rest of society were like you, there would be corpses from end to end of London. And what of those poor soldiers? Maimed and hobbled and on a pension of sixpence a day. The whole of life is compromise. You take what the Good Lord has handed you and make the most of it. Look at you! You are beautiful and titled and well fed and well gowned. Come to think of it,' he went on cheerfully, 'you ought to be ashamed of yourself.'

Jane looked at him steadily, a high colour on her cheeks. 'I must think about what you have just said.' And she turned her gaze away from him and looked across the gardens.

It was just as well for her that Sir Philip's attention had been caught by the charms of a buxom waitress. He raised his quizzing-glass and for the moment forgot about his companion.

Jane struggled for words to explain why she had tried to commit suicide. How could she explain the cruel reality of being isolated in her father's mansion from any normal life? The only servant to ever show her any kindness, her nurse, had been dismissed. Her aunt, the earl's sister, was mostly in residence and ignored Jane as if she did not exist. Jane's young life had been ordered by the cruel tyranny of her governess. And having escaped from home burdened with guilt, lost in a strange world outside her 'prison,' she had felt without hope.

She felt a burning sensation of pure rage at this horrible old man opposite who was ogling the waitress. 'How dare you, sir!' she cried. 'How dare you mock me?'

Sir Philip reluctantly transferred his gaze from the waitress. 'I wasn't mocking you. I just got tired of seeing you mewing and whimpering.'

'Have you considered what my plight will

be when my father finds me?'

Sir Philip sighed. 'He hasn't found you yet, and when he does, you've got all my soft-hearted friends to fight for you. Get it through your pretty head, you are not alone any more. Start living! Wake up! Drink your tea and let me feast my eyes on that shapely waitress.'

Jane glared at him but he appeared to have forgotten her again.

The sun continued to shine, and the river running at the foot of the gardens sparkled in the sun.

Still fuming and fretting over what Sir Philip had said to her, she turned her attention to the other people in the tea-garden.

And then a tall man entered the gardens with a stately lady on his arm. He was extremely handsome in a rakish and dissipated way. He had golden hair curling under a beaver hat. His clothes were beautifully tailored and his Hessian boots shone like the sun. He had broad shoulders and a trim waist and excellent legs. His eyes were very blue and heavy-lidded, which gave his mobile face a mocking look.

The lady was treating him with cold disdain, something which seemed to amuse him.

And then her voice, clear and carrying, reached Jane's ears. 'Is this your idea of entertainment, Monsieur le Comte? To take me to a common tea-garden and place me among common people?'

The comte's eyes ranged lazily about the garden and fell on Jane and widened slightly. Jane tried to look away, as she knew she ought, but felt trapped by that blue gaze. The lady with the comte followed his gaze and looked at Jane as well. Then she got to her feet. 'Take me home,' she ordered sharply. 'This place is a confounded bore.'

The comte dutifully rose to his feet. He bowed in Jane's direction and swept off his hat. The lady walked out of the tea-garden, her head held high. The comte flashed Jane a comical, rueful look and followed her.

Sir Philip's waitress disappeared indoors to the kitchen and he turned to Jane. He saw her face was flushed and her large eyes sparkling.

'You're still in a rage,' he said in a kind voice. 'I don't mind. Angry people don't try to top themselves. I'll take you back.'

The Comte de Mornay greeted his friend, Jamie Ferguson, in a coffee house in Pall Mall later that day.

53

'Sit down, mon ami,' he said, pulling out a chair with his foot. 'I am in love.'

'Again?' said Jamie with a grin. He was a tall, thin man with a clever, fox-like face, pale green eyes and sandy hair. 'What happened to the fair Clarissa?'

'I took her to a tea-garden in Chelsea.'

'What were you about? Only the best will do for Clarissa Vardey. What was wrong with Gunter's or the Poor Relation?'

'I knew she would not like it,' said the comte. 'I had begun to take her to unfashionable places. But although she did not like the tea-garden, I knew I could not move her from my side. So I used my most lethal weapon on her.'

'That being?'

'I told her I had lost all my money on 'Change.'

'She surely did not believe you!'

'Oh, but she did. I explained most carefully that the reason she had been recently subjected to the indignity of meeting me in such low places was because I could not afford anything higher. And just in case she might not believe me, I explained that she could help my life considerably by giving me back the diamond-and-sapphire necklace I gave her for her birthday. She took

54

fright and went back to her husband like any good wife should.'

'So what is this about love?' asked Jamie, amused.

'While we were in the tea-gardens, I saw the most beautiful creature in the world. A face to dream about. She was with some old rip, her father or uncle, no doubt.'

'Or her protector,' said Jamie cynically.

'Never! She had an untouched air about her. I must find her again. She was exquisitely gowned, I mean gowned like a lady. And young. Not yet twenty.'

Jamie laughed. 'This I find hard to believe. You always court married matrons so that you never need to have any fear of marriage.'

'There was something very special about her. Tiens! When our eyes met, I could hardly drag mine away.'

'So when do you meet this paragon again?'

The comte spread his hands in a Gallic gesture of resignation. 'Who knows? Perhaps when the Season begins, I shall find her.'

'Are you so sure she will be there?'

'Her clothes were of the best.'

'She could be the daughter of a rich Cit.'

'The old gentleman with her was no Cit. In fact, I could almost swear I had seen him before.'

'You will amaze the hopeful mamas at the Season if you decide to put in an appearance. They've been after you for years.'

'I am thirty-two, old but not in my dotage.'

Jamie looked at him with affection. 'I always wonder why you never married.'

'Too busy having fun, too busy making the money. My feckless parents, God rest their souls, escaped the Terror with only their jewels. As soon as I came of age, I took what was left and gambled on the Stock Exchange, to great effect, as you know. It was my pleasure to take them out of that sordid lodging-house in North London and transfer them to a life of comfort in the West End.'

Jaime shook his head. 'I still don't know how you became so wealthy so quickly. You would occasionally disappear for months on end and then reappear, more plump in the pocket than before.'

'Business acumen,' drawled the comte. 'But you are not married yourself, hein? How do you account for that?'

Jamie sighed theatrically. 'A broken heart. But you know about that. When we first became friends five years ago, it was the very first thing I told you.'

'Ah, yes, Miss Fiona of the Highlands, who

preferred a Scottish lord double her years and a life in a draughty castle. Mark this, my friend, she has probably got the chilblains all over, elbows like nutmeg graters and a red nose from drinking strong spirits to keep out the cold.'

'Oh, I forgot about her this age. She comes to London with her husband, Lord Dunwilde, for the Season.'

'And you will break her heart in revenge? That is what always happens in the romances.'

Jamie flushed guiltily because that was exactly what he dreamt of doing. 'Fiddle,' he said aloud. 'I shall join you at the Season and together we will hunt down your beauty.'

Harriet, Duchess of Rowcester, sat in the 'staff' sitting room and looked about her with pleasure. 'How good it is to be back,' she exclaimed.

'And how good to see you in looks,' said Lady Fortescue. 'We are so sorry about the death of your child. I lost all mine, one after another. But life goes on and you are still young and strong. You will have more.'

'Enough of my problems,' said Harriet hurriedly. 'When do I meet this Lady Jane?'

'We just call her Jane – Jane North. Jack

has gone to fetch her. She is very beautiful, yes, but so downcast and sad that you may find the idea of sponsoring her a hopeless task. How was she today, Sir Philip?'

'Less dull than usual,' said Sir Philip. 'We went to the tea-gardens in Chelsea and you should see the waitress there. What shoulders!'

'Spare the ladies,' complained the colonel. 'If you spent the time ogling some waitress, then I have no doubt Jane will be more in the megrims than usual – if that is possible.'

Jack opened the door and Jane made her entrance. She was wearing one of her new gowns of pale blue muslin cut low at the neck. Her glossy hair was elaborately dressed.

Head held high, she looked around the room and then her eyes fell on Sir Philip. 'I have thought about your strictures, sir,' she said, her eyes flashing, 'and I take leave to tell you you are an insensitive toad.'

She then stared around in surprise as Miss Tonks began to giggle helplessly. The colonel and Lady Fortescue were laughing openly, as was Mr Davy. Sir Philip had a malicious grin on his face.

The colonel clapped Sir Philip on the shoulder. 'You've done it, Philip. She's come to life.'

'Enough! Enough!' said Lady Fortescue. 'Jane, my dear, come here and make your curtsy to Her Grace, Harriet, Duchess of Rowcester.'

Bewildered by the response to her acid remark to Sir Philip, Jane nonetheless took in the beautiful and elegant figure of the duchess for the first time. She curtsied low. 'I beg your humble pardon, Your Grace, I did not know there was anyone else present.'

'You may call me Harriet and I shall call you Jane. We shall no doubt be a great deal in each other's company during the Season.'

'The Season, Your ... Harriet?'

'Did Miss Tonks not tell you? I am to bring you out. We shall have such fun.'

'Fun,' echoed Jane, and then she sat down suddenly and began to cry. Harriet, suddenly overcome with longing for her dead child and absent husband, began to cry as well.

Sir Philip marched to the door. 'If this is your idea of fun, then I am going to Limmer's to get drunk!'

THREE

It is charming to totter into vogue.
HORACE WALPOLE

The next day Jane could hardy believe that she was going to have a Season after all. Not that her opinion had been asked. Harriet appeared to consider the matter settled and this beautiful duchess did not seem to think it at all odd that she would be chaperoning a fraud. Perhaps as she had previously worked at the Poor Relation and had probably been subjected to all sorts of adventures, the unusual to her had become everyday.

Jane stopped her packing, for Harriet's carriage was to arrive in an hour's time to take her to the duchess's town house in Park Lane.

She walked to the window and opened it and leaned out and looked down into Bond Street. It was early afternoon and the Bond Street loungers were just starting to go on the strut. A gentleman with a club-foot was heading in the direction of Gentleman Jackson's Boxing Saloon. Jane felt her interest quicken. Could this, then, be the famous Lord Byron? It was well known that Lord Byron, like other gentlemen of the *ton*, took boxing lessons. The art of boxing was considered a must for any gentleman of fashion. Thomas Assheton Smith, when Master of the Quorn, after a battle in Leicester Street with a six-foot coal-heaver, clamped raw steak on both black eyes and sent his defeated opponent a five-pound note for being the best man who had ever stood up to him. Some foreigners landing at Dover were amazed to see a Lord of the Treasury, also just arrived whose ministerial box had been taken away from him by customs-men, lashing out with his fists to regain it. Bottom, that quality in which Sir Philip had found Jane so notably lacking, was highly prized during the Regency.

After the man she believed might be Lord Byron had disappeared, her attention was caught by three dandies walking arm in arm along the pavement, indifferent to the passers-by whom their stately progress was crowding into the kennel. They were formidable figures with their wide-brimmed glossy hats, their spotless white starched cravats so tight and high that the wearers could scarcely look down or turn their heads, their exquisitely cut coats worn wide open to display waistcoats – from left to right – of buff, yellow and rose. Then there were the skin-tight pantaloons, or 'Inexpressibles,' gathered up into a wasp-waist; the fobs, jewels, chains and spotless gloves; the white-thorn cane to hint at the lands from which their incomes derived; and the wonderfully made boots whose surfaces shone like black glass.

Outside the perfumer's opposite, a carriage was setting down a fashionable lady. Like a lot of her peers, the high-waisted fashions gave her a sort of hoisted-up look. She glanced up at the hotel and Jane, drawing back a little so as not to be noticed watching, saw that her face had an odd look, a cross between vacuity and insolence. She was soon to learn that this was the London look.

Her thoughts were in a jumble. She could not quite believe that, for the present time anyway, she was safe from tyranny. But she would need to be very brave and enjoy as much of each day as she could. For sooner or later her father would find her and bring with him the terrible Miss Stamp, and Jane shuddered at the thought of the dreadful punishments that woman would enjoy meting out.

She stayed so long buried in her thoughts that the chiming of the clock finally alerted her to the time, and she scrambled through the rest of her packing.

John, who, with his wife Betty, was personal servant to the hotel owners, came to carry down her trunks, her luggage having been augmented now by the clothes Lady Fortescue had ordered for her. Jane wished Miss Tonks had decided to come with her. She wondered what Harriet was really like.

'I have decided,' said Harriet, 'to start nursing the ground. To that effect, I think we should make calls. As Duchess of Rowcester, I am welcomed everywhere, a fact I still find strange, for when I was cook at the hotel, a Cit's family would not even have entertained me.'

Jane looked at the calm and beautiful face opposite, at the beauty of the duchess's jewels and the elegance of her gown and said, 'I cannot imagine you working in a kitchen.'

Harriet laughed. 'I was very good at it, but I must admit I was relieved when Sir Philip found a chef to replace me.'

'You are very good to do this for me,' said

63

Jane. 'I ... I do not deserve such kindness. I tried to take my own life.'

'Well, to be sure you must have been at your wits' end.'

'It must seem very odd to you who have so much courage that someone could be so cowardly as to contemplate suicide.'

Harriet's green eyes suddenly filled with tears and she turned her head away.

Jane rushed and knelt at her feet and took her hands in her own. 'What is it? You must not cry.'

Harriet took out a handkerchief and dried her eyes. 'I lost my daughter. She died of typhoid. I was distraught. I still grieve. Yes, I do know what it is like to want to take one's own life.'

'The duke, your husband?' said Jane. 'He is not with you?'

'He is gone to Italy to attend a funeral. We ... we have become estranged over the death and it is all my fault. When my Emily died, I felt all love, all caring, all affection draining out of me. Dear me, Jane, and I am supposed to be entertaining you. I do not know what came over me.'

But Jane's sudden sharp concern for her hostess had made her temporarily forget her own troubles. 'If the idea of attending events

64

at the Season is too much for you, Harriet,' she said, 'we could still contrive to have a pleasant but quiet time and we could talk often about your poor Emily. One must have someone to talk to.' She sighed. 'I never did, you see, and that is perhaps what magnified all my problems out of proportion.'

Harriet smiled. 'Rise. Or you will get a cramp kneeling at my feet. No, a few balls and parties will entertain me. We shall go on a call to a certain Mrs Haggard, a friend of my husband, who is *bon ton*. She has a daughter, Frances, to puff off, and so she will know all the eligibles. How are your water-colours? One must have a portfolio to show gentlemen callers.'

'I believe my painting is adequate. Painting, books and music were my only escape.'

'Pianoforte?'

'Again, quite good, I think.'

'And your singing voice?'

'Not good at all, I am afraid.'

'But you know how to receive and entertain gentlemen?'

'I have had experience of entertaining my father's friends, yes.'

'I understand from my friends that you are pretending to be staying with some old nurse and that you have forwarded money to her and letters for your father.'

'Yes, they are most kind. I must find some way to repay them for their generosity. My new gowns were so expensive, they made me blink.'

'But you must have been aware of the high cost of dressmaking?'

Jane shook her head. 'A dressmaker came from the nearby town at home to fit me. The gowns were made and the bills sent to my father.'

'Never mind,' said Harriet. 'There is always some way to repay the poor relations!'

'The hotel owners? And yet they appear to be wealthy.'

'They lived through a series of adventures, I can assure you. Since my marriage I have been kept informed of everything that has happened by Miss Tonks and Lady Fortescue. Now you must change and look your best.'

Jane went thoughtfully off to her room. She found a lady's-maid waiting for her who introduced herself as Mary. 'You are Her Grace's lady's-maid?' said Jane. 'Perhaps you should attend to your mistress first.'

Mary curtsied. 'I am your lady's-maid, Miss North. I was elevated in station today from housemaid. If it please you, miss, I am perhaps not as practised as most lady's-maids, but I am willing to learn.'

Jane submitted to her ministrations, her brain in a turmoil. So much had happened to her emotions. She remembered her fury at Sir Philip and blushed. All he had spoken was the truth. How selfish she had been! And now here was Harriet, despite her great grief giving up time and money to bring out an impostor. But it was not Sir Philip's criticisms which had brought Jane to life, but her deep concern for her hostess. Wrapped all her young life in her own misery, Jane had never been able to look out from her confined world and see any misery in others.

She resolved to do her very best to please this Mrs Haggard. She could only hope the lady would like her.

But from the moment she entered Mrs Haggard's saloon and made her curtsy, her heart sank. Mrs Haggard's cold, rather bulbous eyes raked her up and down. Then she delivered herself of a contemptuous sniff before turning away to introduce her daughter, Frances. Frances was a small girl with a great quantity of brown frizzy hair, a snub-nose, and a large mouth. There were four other matrons in the room. Harriet drew Jane forward and introduced her. Hard eyes stared at Jane's beautiful face. One of the matrons only gave her two fingers to shake.

'Come and look at my sketches,' said Frances.

Jane obediently followed her to the end of the long, dim room, leaving Harriet, the matrons and Mrs Haggard in a little island formed of chairs and a table next to the fireplace.

A desire to do her best for Harriet prompted Jane to say in a low voice, 'Did I do something wrong, Miss Haggard? I appear to be the subject of intense disapproval.'

'Of course you are,' said Frances. 'You do not have to look at these boring old drawings. I simply want to talk. It is because you are beautiful and that means you are competition. The others there also have daughters to bring out. Any moment now, Mama will bring out the list of eligibles and the others will take notes and know to whom to send a card to a ball or rout. But you look quite clever as well. Are you?'

And Jane, reflecting on what she now saw as her gross lack of gratitude in that she had tried to commit suicide and then, having been saved from death, had not put herself out very much in any way to thank her benefactors, said, 'I think I am rather stupid.'

'Well, that shows you are clever. Only very clever people can afford to say they are stupid. I need your help.'

'In what way, Miss Haggard?'

'Call me Frances, for we are going to be such friends.'

'We are?' Jane was half amused, half taken aback.

'Oh, yes. We must combine forces. I have worked it out very carefully. The minute I saw you, I thought: If I make a friend of her and keep close to her at balls and parties, she will attract the gentlemen, and as she cannot dance with them all, they will be obliged, through politeness, don't you see, to turn to me and ask me.'

'Your remarks are very flattering, Frances, but I do not consider myself beautiful.'

'Oh, but you are. You could do with a little animation. I know it is fashionable to be poker-faced, but I notice that young ladies with animation are considered attractive. I note these things, don't you know, and write them all down. Then I study my notes as a student studies his professor's teachings.'

'Do the other ladies go to such efforts?' asked Jane.

'What are you talking about, Frances?' called Mrs Haggard.

69

Frances jerked open a portfolio. 'Miss North is advising me on how to better my technique with putting a wash on paper, Mama.'

'Very well.' Mrs Haggard turned back to her guests.

'No, I do not think so,' said Frances, turning back to Jane. 'I hope not, for then I will have the *edge*, don't you see? I have already selected my beau. I saw him driving in the Park and asked Mama who he was. She said he was a Mr Jamie Ferguson and not at all suitable.'

'In what way?'

'He is reported to be in love with a Scottish lady, Lady Dunwilde, and he is best friend of the rackety Comte de Mornay, who goes about breaking hearts and never getting married. I made a sketch of him. See, I have hidden it between the one of this boring cottage and this dreary tree.'

The rather foxy features of a gentleman looked up at Jane.

'You are awfully good,' said Jane.

'Yes, I am, aren't I? But Mama does not know that. Ladies should not be clever at anything to do with art. They are expected to confine themselves to pretty sketches. So this, then, is Mr Ferguson. So you must flirt

70

with him and attract him to your side and then spurn him quite dreadfully so that he will turn to me for consolation. He is usually with the French comte. This is he.'

She slid out another sketch. Jane looked down at the man she had seen in the tea-gardens in Chelsea. 'You do not approve of him?' she asked Frances, for the comte's handsome face had a sinister cast.

'No, I do not. How can Mr Ferguson consider marriage with such a friend always near him? She lowered her voice even more and leaned forward so that her frizzy hair tickled Jane's cheek. 'You will help me, will you not?'

Jane laughed and Harriet, at the other end of the room, turned and smiled. A small triumph to report to her friends at the Poor Relation.

'I think you are a romantic. You have written a play in which I shall attract this Mr Ferguson, make him fall in love with me, then jilt him so that he turns to you. I do have it correct?'

'Oh, yes, and a very sensible idea it is, too.'

'I fear you overestimate my looks. Perhaps we should just begin to be friends and then see what happens when the Season begins.'

Frances opened her brown eyes to their

widest. 'Fiddle! We must seize the moment, Jane. We must hunt down Mr Ferguson *before* the Season begins. Mama is even beginning to mark down a Mr Thompson as a suitable beau, and he is only nineteen and has pimples.'

'And how can two young ladies hunt down a gentleman? We cannot go to a coffee house or yet to his club.'

'I've found out where he lives. He has lodgings in Curzon Street. We could drive out, so respectably, don't you see, and alight to look at the shops. If we see him, I will faint, and you will call to him for assistance.'

'Frances, that is very bold. I should feel very embarrassed.'

'Would you? But will you drive out with me tomorrow at three just the same?'

'Yes, I would like that. Unless Her Grace has other plans for me, of course.'

'That was useful,' said Harriet as they drove home. 'You will be invited by Mrs Haggard to her daughter's come-out, and two of the other ladies will send cards to various functions.'

'I do not think Mrs Haggard likes me.'

'Of course not,' said Harriet. 'Nor did the

others, not with daughters to bring out. How could they? You will put the other young misses in the shade. I told them roundly that to exclude a beauty who could be guaranteed to draw the gentlemen was sheer folly, and so they finally agreed with me.'

'How ruthless all this is,' said Jane wistfully. 'Not at all like books.'

'But you would not like life to be like books, or rather, romances. Were it so, you would spend your time being frightened by headless spectres and carried off to ruined Italian castles by foreign counts. You appear to have formed a friendship with Frances Haggard.'

'I like her.' Jane debated whether to tell Harriet about Frances's mad ideas of pursuit, but then said instead, 'Frances wishes me to go out with her tomorrow at three.'

'I have no plans for you. Do you wish the carriage?'

'No, I thank you; as we left, Frances said she would call on me.'

'Then you may send one of the footmen, when we get home, with a note to tell her that you may go. I myself will call on my friends at the Poor Relation. They are so tranquil now. No plots or plans or upsets. Such a relief!'

73

At the hotel Mr Davy, whose job apart from debt-collecting was to oversee the running of the coffee room, was rarely at his post these days. An excellent manager called Jobson, hired by Sir Philip, saw to everything. He had therefore decided to spend a pleasant after-noon taking Miss Tonks out on a drive. And so it was Sir Philip who was told the news that Jobson had requested the day off to go to his aunt's funeral.

'Send for Davy,' he told Jack, the footman, who had brought him the news.

'Mr Davy, sir, has gone on a drive with Miss Tonks.'

'Mountebank,' snarled Sir Philip. 'Oh, well, I may as well see to it myself.'

He went down to the coffee room in a bad temper. Now if there was one thing Sir Philip loathed, it was a Bond Street lounger, that breed of man who drawled at the top of his voice, insulted the waiters, stared at the ladies and complained about everything. Sir Philip was not only angry, he was tired. He had been up half the night drinking at Lim-mer's, and his head throbbed and his old eyes burned.

He went into the coffee room. John, one of the waiters, took him aside. 'We have a gentleman, sir, who is ogling the ladies and behaving in an offensive manner. He is with, I believe, a foreign gentleman.'

'Walk outside with me a little,' said Sir Philip. 'I will deal with them presently.'

When they were outside in the hall under the great chandelier, which Sir Philip had blackmailed his nephew into giving him, he said testily, 'Has Davy shown his nose in the coffee room today at all?'

'No, Sir Philip,' said John. 'But Mr Jobson is usually always at his post. Today is the first time he has been absent.'

'That's no excuse,' said Sir Philip. 'It's Mr Davy's *duty* to see that all is well before he goes jauntering off around the Town like the gentleman he isn't. I suppose I had better go and get rid of the rats myself.'

'I must go down to the kitchens and bring up some more cakes,' said the waiter, and made his escape.

But in the brief time during which Sir Philip had been talking to the waiter, neither of them had noticed the gentlemen who had been creating the fuss in the coffee room leaving, and that Mr Jamie Ferguson and his friend, the Comte de Mornay, had taken their place.

'So this is the famous Poor Relation,' said the comte, looking around. 'It is kind of you to entertain me, Jamie. I do not know why I have not visited here before. They call it the marriage market and joke that any gentleman daring to enter its portals will shortly find himself engaged to be married to one of the servants.'

'There are no dazzlers here,' said Jamie, looking around. 'Only matrons. And there is a dreadful-looking old gentleman in an impossible wig and with his false teeth bared approaching us.'

Sir Philip stopped at their table.

'I must ask you to leave,' he said.

The comte leaned back in his chair and stared at Sir Philip.

'Why?'

'The ladies present find your manner offensive as do I.'

'Look here, madman,' said the comte in a gentle voice, 'get you back to Bedlam before I get someone responsible in this hotel to throw you out.'

'I,' said Sir Philip wrathfully, 'am Sir Philip Sommerville, owner of this hotel. Get out.'

The comte smiled lazily. 'Shan't.'

'Shall!' shouted Sir Philip. 'I am weary of clods like you, sir. We do not allow boorish manners here.'

'But you do. You do,' said the comte gleefully, 'because you've got plenty of them yourself.'

Beside himself with rage, Sir Philip spat at the table and his false teeth flew out and lay between the bemused comte and Jamie, winking in the light.

Sir Philip snatched them up and stuffed them in his mouth and ran out. 'Help! Help!' he shouted in the hall. The servants came running. John, the waiter, appeared up from the kitchens carrying a tray laden with cakes.

Lady Fortescue and the colonel emerged from the office. 'Sir Philip, what is the matter?'

He began an incoherent rant in which the perfidy of Mr Davy and the sheer evil of the pair in the coffee room were mixed up, ending with a shriek of 'Call the watch! Call the militia!'

But John, who had placed his tray of cakes on a side-table just inside the door of the coffee room, took a quick glance around and came back crying, 'They have gone!'

Sir Philip strode to the door of the coffee room and glared inside. 'They're still there!'

'Not *them*, sir. An uncouth lout of a gentleman and his German companion.'

Sir Philip clutched his wig and groaned.

'You had best go away,' said Lady Fortescue, 'and leave this to myself and the colonel. You have obviously made a stupid mistake. Just go away. Lie down. You look terrible.'

'Now what?' asked the comte, as he saw the stately figure of Lady Fortescue approaching on the arm of Colonel Sandhurst. 'It looks as if the old boy has summoned an equally geriatric couple to abuse us.'

Lady Fortescue curtsied and the colonel bowed. 'We apologize on behalf of our partner, Sir Philip Sommerville,' said Lady Fortescue. 'I am Lady Fortescue. This is Colonel Sandhurst.'

Both Jamie and the comte rose to their feet and bowed.

'Pray be seated, gentlemen,' said Lady Fortescue. The colonel drew out a chair for her and she sat down opposite them. The colonel joined her.

The comte introduced himself and Jamie, which involved everyone standing up again, the gentlemen bowing and Lady Fortescue curtsying.

'Now, Monsieur le Comte,' began Lady Fortescue, 'you and Mr Ferguson here have been victims of a sad misunderstanding. We are often plagued with uncouth Bond Street loungers. Sir Philip was told there was such a one in the coffee room, accompanied by a foreign gentleman. By the time Sir Philip entered to evict the nuisances, they had gone and you had arrived. We can only offer you our deepest apologies and assure you that such a mistake will not happen again.'

'Apology accepted,' said the comte. 'May I say, Lady Fortescue, that perhaps in future you should be sent to deal with any trouble, for the dignity of your presence and the stateliness of your mien would trounce even the most hardened lout.'

Lady Fortescue bowed and for a moment the ghost of the beautiful flirtatious girl she had once been showed behind the mask of paint and wrinkles on her face. Jamie noticed the way the colonel caught that look and the way he scowled.

Lady Fortescue turned and nodded to the waiter, who came hurrying up. 'Coffee and cakes for these gentlemen, John,' she said majestically. 'Do not present them with the bill. Their entertainment is our pleasure.'

John hurried off and Lady Fortescue smiled at the comte. 'Furthermore, you may have heard our cuisine is excellent. You may dine in our hotel any evening you want, as our guests, of course.'

'Too kind,' said Jamie. 'It is the talk of London, Lady Fortescue, of how you and your companions have made a success of business.'

'We have been fortunate,' said the colonel. He gave a little sigh. 'After this Season, we can sell and return to our rightful places in society.' He took Lady Fortescue's hand in his own. 'Lady Fortescue and I plan to settle down.'

'Congratulations, sir.' The comte was touched at this sight of elderly devotion, but it appeared that Lady Fortescue was not amused. She drew her hand away and said sharply, 'We have not yet made up our minds what we plan to do.'

The colonel looked like a sad old dog. The comte said quickly, 'You are very kind, and Mr Ferguson and I would be delighted to be your guests one evening.'

Lady Fortescue parted her thin rouged lips in a smile. 'Here is your coffee. We shall leave you. Again, our apologies.'

The comte and Jamie rose again and bowed. 'Think no more of it, dear lady,' said Jamie. 'All is forgiven.'

But Sir Philip Sommerville, watching sourly from the door of the coffee room, had no intention of ever forgiving this comte for his insolence.

The following day Frances and Jane drove out, accompanied by a footman. The day was fine and Jane was enjoying Frances's company as they were set down at various shops in Pall Mall and then Oxford Street to examine the wares. Jane was just beginning to hope that Frances had given up any mad ideas of running this Mr Ferguson to earth when to her dismay she found their carriage turning into Curzon Street.

'There is a very good perfumer's here,' said Frances lightly. 'I have a mind to buy a bottle of scent.' She called to the coachman to set them down.

As they were about to enter the shop, everything seemed to happen at once. Frances looked along the street and spied Jamie and the comte walking along arm in arm. Sir Philip at that moment emerged from the perfumer's and stood watching.

'Here he comes,' he heard Frances whisper. Sir Philip immediately recognized Jane. He saw her companion put her hand to her brow and begin to sway. Sir Philip recognized the well-known signs of a lady about to pretend to faint so that the gentleman she had her eye on would run and catch her in his arms.

He would have let the comedy proceed

had he not recognized the comte and Jamie.

He quickly stepped forward, just before both gentlemen came up to the ladies. Frances was swaying artistically. With a look of unholy glee on his face, Sir Philip darted forward and caught her in his arms.

'Sir Philip!' cried Jane, blushing with embarrassment.

'Can we be of assistance?' asked the comte. Frances opened her eyes and looked up into the tortoise-like features of Sir Philip Sommerville, gasped and tried to struggle free, but Sir Philip had her in a surprisingly strong grip.

'There is nothing you can do, gentlemen,' said Sir Philip. 'This poor young lady has the vapours and should be taken home immediately. Hey, sirrah!' – to the footman. 'Help me get your mistress to her carriage.'

Fuming inwardly, Frances submitted to being bundled into the carriage. Sir Philip leered up at her. 'You should stay at home if you're poorly. If I had not been on the scene, you might have found yourself in the arms of some mountebank or counter-jumper.'

'Dreadful old man,' said the comte. 'Come along, Jamie.'

Both men strolled off. Jane sharply ordered the coachman to drive on. Sir Philip swept off his hat and gave them a mocking bow.

'Who,' demanded Frances, fanning herself vigorously, 'was that old toad? He appeared to know you.'

'He is one of the owners of the Poor Relation and a friend of the Duchess of Rowcester.'

'Why did he have to be there at that moment?' demanded Frances.

'Well, Frances, my dear, perhaps it was just as well. I remember a lady at an assembly ball at home saying that London gentlemen were well used to ladies turning their ankles outside their houses or fainting in order to get attention.'

'Why didn't you tell me!'

'I just remembered,' said Jane ruefully. 'Frances, it would be better to wait until the Season, when you will have a chance of meeting him properly.'

'By that time he will have eyes only for that Scotch lady he is reported to be so enamoured of. I am in need of a comforting ice at Gunter's. Coachman. Berkeley Square, if you please.'

'They're going into Gunter's,' remarked Jamie. 'Why did you suddenly decide to follow them?'

'I want to meet that beauty,' said the comte.

Because of the press of traffic, they had been able to stroll after the carriage.

'Take my advice,' said Jamie earnestly, 'and wait for the Season. Informal meetings do not work. Besides, that minx with your beauty staged that faint. Perhaps Sir Philip has charms for the young that we do not possess.'

'Perhaps the target was us,' pointed out the comte.

'Could hardly be us. They don't know us.'

'Still, I am suddenly determined to go to Gunter's,' said the comte. 'En avant!'

FOUR

It is under the trees, it is out of the sun,
In the corner where GUNTER retails a plum
bun.
Her footman goes once, and her footman goes
twice,
Ay, and each time returning he brings her an
ice.

ANONYMOUS

Gunter's was set up in 1757 by the Italian pastry-cook Dominicus Negri, who later took Gunter into partnership 'making and selling all sorts of English, French and Italian wet and dry sweetmeats, Cedrati and Bergamet Chips, and Naples Divolini, at the sign of the Pot and Pineapple in Berkeley Square.' The shop was at number seven on the east side of the square, four doors away from Horace Walpole's house. Gunter's ices were famous, made from a secret recipe. In hot summer weather, it was the custom for ladies to recline in their carriages on the *opposite* side of Berkeley Square from

Gunter's while waiters scurried back and forth across the square with trays of ices. It was also the only place in London before the advent of the Poor Relation's coffee room where a gentleman could be seen alone with a lady in the afternoon.

'So what do we do now?' asked Jamie. 'We cannot very well stroll in after them and sit at the same table.'

'It is she,' said the comte dreamily. 'The lady I saw in the Chelsea gardens.'

'Beautiful, I grant you, but somewhat masklike,' said Jamie. 'Very well. But let's hope Sir Philip does not appear again.'

Frances was just urging Jane to try a white-currant ice when she saw Jane staring beyond her and turned round, blushed and turned back.

'Do not be too forward, Frances,' counselled Jane, who was trying to save herself from embarrassment. The waiter arrived and they gave an order for two white-currant ices.

Then, to Jane's dismay, she found the comte at her side, making an excellent bow. 'Forgive me,' he said, 'but I feel we have met. I am the Comte de Mornay and this is my friend, Mr James Ferguson.'

'I am afraid that we have not met or ever been introduced,' said Jane.

'But I have heard of *you*, Mr Ferguson,' said Frances, sparkling up at him.

Jamie laughed. 'Nothing bad, I trust. Whom do I have the pleasure of meeting?'

'I am Miss Frances Haggard.' Frances held out her hand, which Jamie gallantly kissed. 'And this is my friend, Miss Jane North.'

Both gentlemen bowed. 'May we join you?' asked the comte. 'We are both much concerned about your health, Miss Haggard. We saw you faint in Curzon Street.'

'I am really quite delicate,' said Frances, looking the picture of robust health. 'But by all means, join us.'

Jane flashed her a worried look. Perhaps the ways of ladies in London were more free and easy than those of the provinces, but she felt that Frances was being too bold.

The gentlemen sat down. The waiter returned with the ices. The comte and Jamie ordered sorbets.

'I saw you in the Chelsea tea-gardens with Sir Philip Sommerville,' began the comte, turning to Jane. 'Is he some relative?'

'No, Monsieur le Comte,' said Jane. 'He and the owners of the Poor Relation Hotel are friends of my hostess, the Duchess of Rowcester. I am new to London and he was entertaining me.'

She addressed the table as she spoke, feeling uncomfortable, not wanting to meet his blue gaze.

'Let me tell you about Sir Philip,' said Jamie gaily. He began to tell the story about their experience in the hotel coffee room while Frances laughed – immoderately, Jane thought, picking at her ice and fretting about what on earth to do.

The comte studied her beautiful face and wondered why there was such an air of sadness about her. He had a desire to make her smile. He told several of his best anecdotes and Frances and Jamie laughed appreciatively, but still that beautiful face showed not the slightest trace of animation.

Jane found the comte terrifying. His mocking, glinting eyes that slanted mischievously at her, the splendour of his clothes and jewels, the light, intriguing scent he wore – it all made her feel confused and threatened. She had never dreamt of such a man. The man of her dreams was solid and reliable, more like a father ought to be than a lover.

Harriet, passing in the square outside, recognized the Haggards's footman standing by the carriage and called on her coachman to stop. She learned that 'the ladies' were inside Gunter's. Followed by her maid, she entered the pastry-cook's and stopped short at the sight of Frances and Jane being entertained by two gentlemen.

Jane cast a mute appeal for help at Harriet and Harriet sailed forward. The gentlemen rose to their feet and then there was a great deal of bowing and scraping and curtsying before Harriet said, 'I was not aware that either Miss Haggard or Miss North was acquainted with either of you.'

'We have a mutual friend in Sir Philip Sommerville,' said Jamie.

'Indeed!' Harriet looked him up and down. 'And just exactly on what occasion did Sir Philip introduce you?'

Jamie looked awkward. 'We were not *exactly* introduced but...'

'I thought so,' said Harriet. 'Frances, Jane, come along. Gentlemen, good day.'

They both remained standing while Harriet ushered the girls out of the pastry-cook's. Frances hesitated, half turned and let her handkerchief drop to the ground, and then she hurried out after Harriet and Jane.

'Don't tell Mama,' cried Frances breathlessly. 'They were all that is correct, don't you know.'

'No, I don't know,' said Harriet crossly. She stopped by the Haggard carriage. 'Jane, you are coming home with me. But first, how did this come about? You will ruin your chances at the Season if it gets about that you are in the way of being entertained by the Comte de Mornay. I have heard of that gentleman, and he is a *rake*.'

'Frances felt faint in Curzon Street,' said Jane. 'Sir Philip was there to catch her just as the two gentlemen were passing. They must have seen us go to Gunter's and called to ask how Frances was.'

'Nonetheless, you must never do such a thing again.'

'Please don't tell Mama,' urged Frances again.

Harriet looked at the pleading face under that odd mop of frizzy hair and smiled. 'Not this time. Do not do such a thing again.'

'But Duchess, the comte may have the reputation of a rake, but surely there is nothing against his friend, Mr Ferguson.'

'Not that I know,' said Harriet. 'But if that gentleman wishes to make your acquaintance, then he must do it the usual way through formal channels.'

'So do I return this handkerchief?' asked Jamie with a grin.

'I think the minx is interested in you,'

replied the comte. 'I shall come with you. In that way, I may get a chance to meet the beautiful Miss North again.'

'How do I find out where she lives?'

'Ask Josh, the porter, at the club. He knows the direction of everyone. I would not tell her no-doubt-respectable mama that we sat down with her and I doubt if she will say anything, although that beautiful and stately duchess might. Simply say she dropped it as she was leaving.'

'And when should I call?'

'Leave a space of two days.'

'I hope the duchess isn't there.'

'Why? She is as beautiful as my Miss North.'

'I feel she does not approve of us one bit, my friend.'

But when they called after two days, it was to learn that Miss Frances and her mother, Mrs Haggard, were out on calls.

'That's that,' said Jamie.

'We could drive by the Duchess of Rowcester's,' pointed out the duke, 'and see if the Haggard carriage is there.'

'And what does the Haggard carriage look like? Will it have a crest?'

The comte smiled lazily. 'I neither know

nor care. My tiger can quiz the coachmen outside the duchess's residence.'

The house in Park Lane was still protected from what had all too recently been Tyburn Way, where the condemned were taken to the gallows, followed by the mob, and so the entrance to the house was in Park Street. Both men waited while the comte's diminutive tiger questioned the coachmen of several carriages waiting outside. He came back to say that various ladies were calling on the duchess, among them Mrs Haggard and her daughter.

'So,' said the comte, 'in we go.'

Jamie hesitated. 'We do not really have an excuse.'

'Of course we do, mon ami. That handkerchief which Miss Frances so carefully let fall. Courage. I shall look on Miss North again.'

Harriet studied their visiting cards in dismay. She was about to tell the butler that she was 'not at home,' but a Mrs Bletchley, a friend of Mrs Haggard, said eagerly, 'You look dismayed. Who has called?'

'Monsieur le Comte de Mornay and his friend Mr Ferguson,' said Harriet.

'Oh, do have them up,' cried Mrs Bletchley. 'The comte is such a rattle.'

'You are surely not interested in a rattle for your Sarah,' said Harriet.

'Fiddle. This French comte is ridiculously wealthy and must settle down sometime. I beg you, dear Duchess, show them up.'

'Very well,' said Harriet but she was aware of Frances's shining eyes and the rigidity of Jane's face. Sarah Bletchley had run to the mirror to pat her curls. She was a dumpy little girl, and yet, to Frances's suddenly jealous eyes, she appeared to have hitherto unnoticed charms.

The ladies all sat in a half-circle round the fire. The two gentlemen entered. There were classes in Bond Street to instruct gentlemen of the *ton* in the correct way to 'break the circle,' as it was called. It was considered a superior grace to know how to enter a drawing room, to penetrate the circle, to make a slight inclination as you walked around it, to make your way to your hostess unruffled, with your hat under your arm, with your stick, your gloves, and, possibly, since it was all the rage, an enormous muff. Gentlemen also took lessons in how to move. Gentlemen did not just walk, they glided. Fashion was all. There was even a whole chapter in a book on etiquette entitled, 'How to take off your hat and replace it.' The comte acquitted himself with elegance; Jamie, passably.

'To what do we owe the pleasure of this visit?' asked Harriet when all the introductions had been made and all the bowing and curtsying were over.

Jamie produced the handkerchief and presented it to Frances. 'You dropped this in Gunter's the other day.'

Frances flashed a guilty little look at her mother before she smiled and took it. 'How very kind of you, sir.'

But Mrs Haggard had been doing some quick arithmetic in her head. Mr Ferguson was not amazingly rich like this French comte, but tolerably well off. 'Show Mr Ferguson your portfolio, Frances,' she said.

Frances led James off to the end of the large saloon. With the grace of a dancing master, the comte took a chair, placed it next to Jane and sat down. Harriet watched this anxiously, but Mrs Haggard, on the comte's other side, said, 'Will you be honouring us with your presence this Season, my dear Comte?'

'Yes, I think I shall,' said the comte while he wondered what was wrong with this Miss Jane North. What was causing that aura of sadness?

Mrs Bletchley laughed. 'You will break

hearts as usual and remain just as unwed at the end of this one as you have remained unwed at the end of all the others.'

'How ancient you do make me feel,' said the comte. 'But I may surprise you, madam. It is time I settled down.'

'You amaze us,' giggled Sarah. She hid her face behind her fan, then peeped over it at him. 'You sound as if you have met a lady of your choice.'

'I rather think I have.'

'Tell us,' urged Mrs Bletchley, thinking that Sarah had never looked so well.

'Ah, that is my secret. I fear the lady is not even aware of me.'

For a brief moment his eyes slid to Jane, who was sitting with her hands folded in her lap. Oh, no, thought Harriet. Very unsuitable. Jane needs a steady, reliable man, the kind of man I could take aside and explain her predicament to. Not this frivolous rake. He might even think the irregularity of her situation puts her in the mistress class!

Frances was showing her water-colours to Jamie, who was examining them with his quizzing-glass. Frances amused him. She was such a friendly little thing. 'Do you plan to find a bride at the Season, Mr Ferguson?' asked Frances.

'Alas. I fear I cannot. My heart is not yet mended and the lady who broke it will be at the Season ... with her husband.'

'Ah, Lady Dunwilde,' said Frances.

There is nothing more irritating than finding out that the secret of your heart is public property. Jamie's face darkened. He tucked away the quizzing-glass. 'I have stayed long enough,' he said abruptly.

'I am sorry,' said Frances impulsively. 'I should not have mentioned her name. But I could be of use to you, sir.'

He had begun to turn away from her, but at this he turned back and said in a voice in which irritation and amusement were equally mixed. 'How, my child?'

'I am not a child,' said Frances. 'I merely meant that I could make a confidante of this lady and find out what she thinks of you, don't you know, and if I found out that she cared for you just a little bit, you might feel better about things.'

'You would do that for me?'

'Oh, yes,' said Frances. 'You had best ask Mama if you can take me driving tomorrow and we will discuss strategy.'

He laughed. 'You are a minx and I should not encourage you. But yes, I would dearly like to know what the lady thinks of me.'

'Is she very old?'

'Old? Of course not. She is the same age as myself.'

'The prime of life for you, sir. You are in your early thirties, are you not? But middle-aged for a lady.'

'You are too harsh. I see my friend is ready to leave.' He bowed before Frances, thinking again what a funny-looking little girl she was.

Meanwhile the comte had asked permission to take Jane driving, but Harriet had said firmly that as Jane's wardrobe was not complete, she had to be at home for fittings. The comte looked at Jane's still face for any sign that she might be either relieved or saddened by this decision but came to the conclusion that the mysterious Miss Jane North did not care one way or the other.

'How did you fare?' asked Jamie when the comte drove off.

'Very badly, my friend. I asked her to go driving with me, or rather, I asked the duchess, who refused permission, and the sad Miss North sat with her head bowed, caring neither one way nor t'other.'

'I am taking her little friend, Miss Haggard, on a drive tomorrow, so I will find out more about Miss North for you.'

'Miss Haggard is an engaging child,' said the comte. 'A much healthier pursuit than your mercenary Scotchwoman.'

'She is *not* mercenary.'

'My apologies. It was the title.'

'It was her parents, I am convinced of that. She had no choice in the matter. Miss Haggard has offered her help. She is to become a confidante of my Fiona during the Season and find out if she cares for me a little.'

'This being Miss Haggard's idea?'

'Yes, she is a good-hearted girl.'

And a devious one, thought the comte. But I am not going to put a spoke in her wheel.

Aloud he said, 'Do not quiz her about Miss North. I have lost interest.'

'So soon?'

'There is nothing there to be interested *in*. No sparkle, no wit, no humour.' The comte sounded almost angry.

'And no interest in you?' Jamie grinned. 'Your pride has taken a dent. Hitherto you have only been interested in eager matrons who wish to be unfaithful to their boring husbands. Still, it is not like you to give up so easily.'

'Then you do not know me very well. Who wants to make love to a statue?'

Although some of the following day was taken up with fittings, Jane found there were more calls to make. Harriet was taking her job of bringing Jane out seriously. 'I hope you did not mind me refusing the comte permission to take you driving. He is too old and frivolous for you. You need someone younger and of a serious turn of mind.'

'Yes, I am a trifle dreary, I confess,' said Jane. 'I feel the threatening shadow of my father always looming up behind me. I am so grateful to you, Harriet, for all your kindness, and yet I feel such expense and care are wasted on me. What serious and sober man is going to look on me favourably when he finds that I have been masquerading under another name? What if one of my neighbours who saw me at assemblies at home should turn up at the Season and recognize me?'

'Do you know, I don't think anyone would. No one surely is going to think that the beautiful Miss Jane North, sponsored by the Duchess of Rowcester, is Lady Jane Fremney. They will merely think there is a striking likeness. I have a mind to go out this evening to the Poor Relation and visit my friends. They gather in their own sitting room after dinner and chat. It will remind me of the old days. Would you care to join me? It will not harm your reputation, for who will notice us? It is a very fashionable hotel and they will think we are going to pay court to the prince.'

Jane agreed that, yes, she would like to go, simply because she knew it would please Harriet.

Jamie and the comte made their way to the Poor Relation that evening, the comte saying he had every intention of taking up Lady Fortescue's invitation to a free meal. He also knew it would irritate Sir Philip. Jamie was in good form, having enjoyed his drive with Frances more than he had expected to. She was so easy to talk to, and because they were now conspirators in a way, he did not have to worry about making polite conversation. He had not told Frances anything about the comte's previous interest in Jane, for the comte had declared himself to have lost that interest.

Sir Philip was every bit as annoyed with their appearance as the comte had gleefully anticipated. But the food was excellent and it was amusing to see how Sir Philip, Lady Fortescue and Colonel Sandhurst appeared to serve the prince and his entourage while it was the waiters, in fact, who did all the work.

The prince's mistress kept casting roguish looks in the comte's direction. Before, the comte would have enjoyed the game of flirting back, but for some reason he now thought it would be a rather childish thing to do. To his annoyance, he found his thoughts constantly straying to Jane North. He should not have given up that game so easily, not before he had managed to make her laugh.

He was facing the open door of the dining room and had just finished the pudding when he saw the Duchess of Rowcester and Miss Jane North arriving. They went past his vision in the direction of the stairs.

He saw that Lady Fortescue had noticed the arrivals. She said to the colonel, 'Harriet is here with Jane.' And then the colonel, Sir Philip, and Lady Fortescue left, leaving the waiters to collect the pudding plates and serve the nuts, fruit, wine, and butter at the end of the meal, some people preferring to eat butter with a spoon to finish off their dinner.

'How very curious,' said the comte. 'Miss Jane North and the duchess have just made their entrance and presumably gone upstairs. Lady Fortescue says to that colonel, "Harriet is here with Jane," and then the three owners take their leave. Ah, of course, the Duchess of

Rowcester was once Harriet James, fallen on hard times, and rumour has it did the cooking in the kitchens here. So no doubt she has come to talk over old times. Where? They must have a private room somewhere, some parlour to which they retire.'

'You are never thinking of going after them!' exclaimed Jamie. 'Not the done thing. Not convenable, mon brave.'

'Your French accent is appalling. Why not? It is our duty to thank the owners for this free meal and assure them all is forgiven. All very conventional.'

Jane, suddenly shy at finding herself back amongst the very people who had saved her life, sat next to Miss Tonks on the sofa. Sir Philip had just summoned Despard the cook, under the orders of Lady Fortescue. The prince, in raptures as usual over the excellence of Despard's cooking, had given ten guineas to Sir Philip to give to the chef. Sir Philip was all for pocketing it, grumbling that a Despard with too much money might be a Despard who would retire, but Lady Fortescue had insisted that the chef be paid.

Despard took the gold, his twisted face lighting in a smile. He would add it to the stack of gold which he had obtained as a bribe from a certain Lady Stanton who had wished him to flee the country and so leave the Poor Relation without their famous chef. Despard had betrayed her to Sir Philip and the rest and had kept the money. He turned and bowed to Harriet and then left.

'So,' said Mr Davy, 'what is the gossip of the day?'

'Our prince is still happy with us and everything goes smoothly,' said Lady Fortescue. 'No upsets or alarms. Does everything go well with you, Harriet?'

'I am assured of several useful invitations for Jane,' said Harriet. 'We had a visit yesterday from the Comte de Mornay and his friend, Mr Ferguson. I believe you experienced a certain difficulty with them here.'

'A misunderstanding,' said Lady Fortescue smoothly as Sir Philip scowled. 'He is, I believe, rich and unmarried. Have you hopes there?'

'No, he is a rattle. Not at all suitable for Jane.'

'Perhaps Miss Jane needs a rattle,' said Mr Davy sympathetically. 'Opposites attract.'

'Like yourself and Miss Sheep Face there?' demanded Sir Philip waspishly.

'Your jealousy of the friendship between Mr Davy and Miss Tonks is becoming tiresome,' snapped Lady Fortescue, seeing poor Miss Tonks's nose turn red with embarrassment.

'I? Jealous...?' Sir Philip was beginning wrathfully when the door opened and the comte and Jamie stood revealed on the threshold.

'My dear sirs,' protested the colonel, walking forward, 'you have strayed into our private quarters.'

'You must forgive us,' said the Comte ruefully. 'We have enjoyed your hospitality and are come to thank you.'

'You're welcome. Good night,' said Sir Philip, who had followed the colonel. He slammed the door in their faces.

'You impossible little toad,' raged Lady Fortescue. 'Now we shall have to invite them in before that comte decides to call you out for such an insult.' She opened the door. 'My apologies, gentlemen. Such a draught of wind. Pray do join us in a dish of tea.'

To Sir Philip's fury, both came in. Mr Davy had crossed to the piano. Miss Tonks followed him saying, 'If you intend to play, then I will turn the music for you.' That left the place on the small sofa next to Jane empty, and so, with an expert flick of his long coat-tails, the comte sat down next to her. To Sir Philip's further fury, the comte handed his hat, cane and gloves to the poor relations' servant, John, a signal that he had every intention of staying longer than the usual ten minutes a formal call was supposed to take.

Lady Fortescue poured tea for the visitors and then turned to Mr Davy. 'Are you going to entertain us, Mr Davy?'

He smiled. 'Miss Tonks and I went to the Wells the other night to see Grimaldi. I was going to sing you one of his comic songs, but then I did not expect us to have such distinguished visitors.'

'Pray do not let us stop you,' said Jamie. 'Grimaldi is the greatest clown ever.'

'Alas, I will have to sing unaccompanied,' said Mr Davy.

'I'll accompany you,' said Sir Philip, startling everyone with his sudden change from bad temper to amiability. He gleefully thought that Davy had gone mad, and a rendition of a vulgar comic song was just the thing to give this comte a disgust of the company. He assumed Jamie was encouraging Mr Davy out of politeness. 'Hum the refrain,' said Sir Philip, rippling his small, well-manicured hands expertly over the keys.

Mr Davy hummed a jaunty refrain. Sir

Philip went through it a couple of times and then Mr Davy began to sing.

The comte looked at him in surprise. The man was an actor, he thought, not knowing that until recently that had been Mr Davy's profession. The song was a simple one, about a man complaining about his bullying wife, but Mr Davy almost *became* Grimaldi as he sang, complete with funny expressions. There came an odd sound from next to the comte. He glanced in surprise at Jane. She had her handkerchief up to her mouth. He realized she was trying not to laugh. Ladies were supposed to emit tinkling chimes or show classical smiles. They were not supposed to laugh out loud. Society, he thought, has taken every natural expression away from us, from walking to laughing to how we eat. And then Jane gave way. She lowered the handkerchief and laughed out loud, and Lady Fortescue, usually rigid when it came to social behaviour, relaxed and laughed as well, half in amusement at Mr Davy's antics, half in delight at Jane's mirth.

By the time Mr Davy had finished, they were all, with the exception of a surprised and disgruntled Sir Philip, helpless with laughter. Mr Davy bowed before the applause and then said cheerfully, 'Now I will sing you a ballad. "The Minstrel Boy."'

'I don't know that,' said Sir Philip, scuttling away from the piano.

'You do, too,' complained Miss Tonks.

'I will sing unaccompanied,' said Mr Davy.

The words of Thomas More's lovely song sounded round the room in a clear tenor voice.

> *'The Minstrel Boy to the war is gone,*
> *In the ranks of death you'll find him;*
> *His father's sword he has girded on,*
> *And his wild harp slung behind him.'*

There was a little respectful silence when he had finished and then applause. Jamie, who was sitting opposite Jane, noticed with a sort of wonder that she had *thawed out,* as he described it to himself. Her large eyes were sparkling and there was a delicate pink bloom on her cheeks.

She heard the comte say, 'You ought to be on the stage, sir,' and then Mr Davy's reply, 'But I was until recently,' and that struck her as funny as well and she laughed helplessly while the comte looked down at her in sudden affection and wanted to take her in his arms.

He set himself to please, and entertained

the company with various anecdotes about the follies of society while Sir Philip glowered and Harriet studied Jane's glowing face and worried about her. This comte was too frivolous, too unstable. All at once, Harriet longed for her husband, who would know exactly what to do. He would surely have reached Milan by now. But how long would it take for a letter to arrive? And what kind of letter? Why had she been so selfishly cold to him? But for the moment she must concentrate on Jane's safety. When the comte and Jamie at last took their leave, Harriet drew Sir Philip aside, waspish Sir Philip who nonetheless had proved so clever in the past at getting them out of scrapes.

'I am anxious about this comte,' she said in a low voice.

'And so you should be,' pointed out Sir Philip. 'His visit tonight was no accident. He is pursuing Lady Fremney.'

'Miss North,' corrected Harriet. 'It is better if we use her new name at all times. I think I need your help, Sir Philip. The comte is highly unsuitable. I am delighted to see Jane has recovered her spirits, but I am determined to find her a suitable beau and the comte is not my idea of a correct and stable gentleman.'

'I'll think o' something. In fact, I'll start now,' said Sir Philip, his pale eyes gleaming as he saw a way to get even with the comte. 'Leave her to me.'

He slid over and jerked his head at Miss Tonks, who was sitting beside Jane on the sofa. She rose after throwing him a suspicious look and went to talk to Mr Davy.

'Good to see you in high spirits,' said Sir Philip.

'Mr Davy is so very clever,' said Jane. 'I wish I had seen him on the stage.'

'Tol rol,' remarked Sir Philip dismissively. 'All these actors can do is perform. But nothing out of the common way. Sort of thing that amuses that French comte. We'll be the talk of London tomorrow.'

'How so?'

'Oh, he is such a gossip. He will rattle on about his unfashionable evening, listening to vulgar songs in an hotel sitting room and make a mock of all of us.'

Jane's eyes widened. 'He is not like that, surely. There is a lightness of character about him, I admit. But he seems a gentleman.'

'Not where the ladies are concerned. That fellow has had more mistresses – you forgive me speaking so plain? – than I have had hot dinners. He is the despair of the Season.

Rich and handsome, I will allow. He occasionally flirts with some gullible young miss, breaks her heart and then goes off to pay court to a flighty matron anxious for an amour.'

Jane thought of the little scene in the tea-gardens. Who had the lady been? A discarded mistress? What a wicked, dismal world it all was. She felt as depressed as she had recently been elated.

'Sir Philip!' Lady Fortescue's voice was sharp. 'What are you saying to Miss North?'

'Just tittle-tattle,' said Sir Philip quickly.

'I have been thinking,' said Harriet on the road home, 'that this comte's attentions cannot do you harm. Despite his reputation, he is accounted a great catch. Perhaps, should he ask again, I will give you permission to go driving with him.'

'I do not want to encourage the attentions of such a man,' said Jane in a low voice.

'As you will. But why?'

'Sir Philip told me of his mistresses, of his reputation.'

Harriet looked at her in dismay. 'I am afraid that was my fault. Seeing you so happy and animated, I thought... Well, in any case, I told Sir Philip to warn you off. I had forgot the sheer crudity of his methods. Oh, dear, I forgot, too, about his resentments. Because he mistook the comte for a yahoo and got himself in disgrace with Lady Fortescue and the colonel, he will now want to get even with this comte. I am sorry, Jane.'

'In any case,' said Jane, striving for a lighter tone, 'I am sure there are safer, more charming gentlemen around. Have you heard from the duke?'

'Not yet,' said Harriet sadly. 'I wonder where he is.'

At that moment, the Duke of Rowcester and his servants were sheltering in a grimy tavern some miles from Milan. They had been forced to take shelter from a violent storm. The duke was seated in a dark corner, drinking a glass of the bitter local wine and thinking about his wife. He tried to remember how cold and distant to him she had been of late but could only remember the vibrant loveliness of her before the tragedy of their daughter's death. In and out of his thoughts came the sounds of rapid French from a couple of men, shielded from his view by the back of a high settle. The duke's French was excellent and he suddenly realized the two men were discussing possible ways to free Napoleon from his prison on Elba. He listened, half irritated, half amused, for Europe seemed to be full of Napoleonic plotters hoping to free their hero. What did another pair matter? And then he heard one say, 'You could go to Elba as a tourist after you have silenced that comte for us.'

'De Mornay has exposed plot after plot,' said the other voice. 'But never fear. He is in London and I shall make sure his death looks accidental.'

At that moment, the duke's valet arrived to say that a bedchamber had been prepared. The duke was conscious of two black figures disappearing out of the inn. He wondered who the plotters were but he was exhausted, and what did two more plotters matter? There had already been attempt after attempt to free the emperor, but all had failed.

It was only as he was falling asleep that he recalled the voices and with a little shock realized that the man speaking fluent French, the one who was going to London, had in fact probably been English. There had been something in the intonation and accent. And only an English tourist could go to Elba, and one of high rank. He decided to write to the authorities in Horse Guards in the morning about what he had overheard. But before that, he would write to his wife.

FIVE

It is impossible, in our condition of Society, not to be sometimes a Snob.
WILLIAM MAKEPEACE THACKERAY

A month had passed and the Season was about to begin. There was a hectic air about society, rather like that of actors before an opening night. Only Jane felt strangely unmoved. It still seemed to her an odd dream in which she was living, and yet the only road to freedom lay through marriage. Often she wished she had money of her own so that she might buy a partnership in the hotel. Her visits to the hotel had ceased, Lady Fortescue saying that although the hotel owners were *bon ton*, some slight taint of trade might stick to Jane were she to be seen socializing with them too often.

Frances, Jane knew, was disappointed because Mr Jamie Ferguson had not come to call. For her part, she was glad she had not seen the comte again. He made her feel ...

uncomfortable. Or rather that was the only way she could explain her feelings about him to herself.

Jane found Frances an agreeable companion because Harriet was often withdrawn and seemed to live for the arrival of the post. And then, on the eve of the Season, Harriet received a letter from her husband. Jane did not know what it contained, only that Harriet looked transformed, radiant. The duke had not bothered to mention overhearing the conspirators. That news he had sent in a separate letter to Horse Guards.

Frances called that afternoon to discuss her coming out with Jane at a ball at Lady Farley's the following evening. Frances was unusually subdued. She had not told Jane that although she had gone to Curzon Street several times during the last month with her maid in the hopes of one glimpse of Mr Jamie Ferguson, she had been unlucky. She was plagued with dreams of this beautiful Scotchwoman, Lady Dunwilde. She had learned that she was in London but had not found anyone to describe her looks to her.

'Do you think Mr Ferguson will be at the ball?' she asked again.

'I do not know,' said Jane. 'Harriet has had a letter from her husband which has put her

in alt. I could ask her to question Lady Farley as to whether Mr Ferguson has been
invited.'

But Frances did not want that. For she suddenly knew if she found out before that ball
that he was not going, then she would not
look forward to the event at all. She had
hoped that he would have called on her to
discuss her plan of making Fiona a confidante, but only friends of her mother came to
call, anxious matrons determined that their
daughters should succeed in the marriage
market.

'I think, dear Jane, that I should just wait
and see. But you must remember to attract
the gentlemen to your side and flirt with Mr
Ferguson and then go off and dance with
someone else so that he will be obliged to ask
me.'

'You rate my looks too highly,' said Jane
ruefully.

'Oh, no.' Frances shook her frizzy hair.
'Don't you dream of some gentleman walking towards you across the ballroom, Jane,
and of you looking up and knowing this is
your future?'

Jane gave a little sigh. She could not tell
Frances that at the back of her mind was
always the dread that she would see her

father walking towards her, followed by Miss Stamp. Romance did not seem to play any part in this London of the early-nineteenth century. The heaths around London were decorated with corpses hanging from gibbets, the town was patrolled by window-smashing mobs, and gentlemen had to know how to defend themselves with stick or dress-sword. London was rich in brothels called bagnios, and in gin-shops where it was possible to get drunk for a penny and dead drunk for twopence. Unlike Frances, Jane read a great number of newspapers and magazines and was more aware of the violent life just outside the carefully protected world in which she lived. Because of her brutish father and his equally brutish friends, she saw the studied tenderness to the ladies of society by the gentlemen as a charade, as mannered as dancing. She thought of the Poor Relation Hotel and had a longing to visit the owners who knew her real name, to talk to them about her fears, the fears she did not want to burden Harriet with because Harriet was still in mourning for her dead child.

'You have gone all sad again,' said Frances. 'There is always a sadness about you, Jane, and you never talk of your family. Do they come to London?'

'No,' said Jane briefly. 'They are in the north. Let us change the subject. Is your gown very pretty, Frances?'

'I will sketch it for you,' said Frances, seizing her drawing-book. Her pencil moved rapidly over the paper. 'It is white muslin, of course, very suitable. Do you not wish we could wear scarlet or something like that? It has quite a low neckline, like so, and little puffed sleeves, but it has a gauze overdress with silver-and-sapphire clasps and *three* flounces at the hem. I am to wear a Juliet cap embroidered with pearls and sequins. My gloves are white kid but do not cover my elbows, which is a pity, for although I treat them nightly with lemon juice and goose grease, they are a trifle rough. And little slippers of white kid with rosettes of white silk.'

'Very fine,' said Jane.

'So what is yours like?'

'Come with me and I will show you.' Jane led the way to her bedroom where her gown was displayed on a dummy by the window. Like Frances's evening gown, it was of white muslin but decorated with a little green sprig and ornamented with a wide green silk sash. 'I have green gloves and green shoes to go with it,' said Jane, 'and green silk flowers for my hair. Do you not think the neckline a trifle low?'

Frances put her head on one side like an inquiring bird and studied the gown with interest. 'I do not think so. Low necklines are all the thing. I do wish these fashions which put the waist under the armpits would be exploded. My one claim to beauty is my tiny waist, but no one ever sees it.' She looked out of the window and down to the street below. 'Do you think it will rain? Oh, my heart. There is my Mr Ferguson walking below with that comte. Is he coming here?'

Jane joined her and looked down. The comte and Jamie were strolling arm in arm. As they came abreast of the duchess's house, Jamie said something to the comte as he looked up, and then both laughed.

About to turn away, because Jane felt that both men were probably joking about the bold misses who tried to accost gentlemen in Curzon Street, she suddenly stiffened and stared down. In a closed carriage on the other side of the street, she could make out the burning eyes of some man. His hat was pulled down over the top part of his face and a scarf up over the lower part. A ray of sunlight flashed on something metal and Jane realized with horror that he was holding a pistol and that that pistol was levelled at the two men walking below. She threw up the window and shrieked, 'Look out!'

The man in the carriage shouted something to his driver, who promptly whipped up his horses and the carriage bowled off.

The comte and Jamie looked up in surprise and then swept off their hats and made low bows. 'What is the matter, Jane?' cried Frances.

'I must tell them.' Jane was quite white. 'Some man was going to shoot them.'

'Capital!' cried Frances, clapping her hands. 'What a ruse!'

But Jane was already out of the room and running headlong down the stairs. A footman leaped to open the front door as she ran across the hall.

'Gentlemen!' cried Jane. 'Monsieur le Comte! You must listen.'

They had begun to move on, but at the sound of her voice they both turned about and hurried back to her.

'What is wrong, Miss North?' asked the comte.

Some fashionables passing by were turning to stare. Jane blushed, aware of how unconventional her behaviour must seem. 'Pray step inside,' she urged, 'and I will explain.'

'Delighted to oblige,' said the comte, his

blue eyes sparkling.

Admiring what she considered Jane's un-expected boldness and improvisation, Fran-ces came down the stairs as they entered the hall.

Jane led them into a rather gloomy saloon on the ground floor which was used for receiving the duke's business callers, such as his agent and his tailor. 'We should be chaperoned, Frances,' said Jane in dismay.

'Leave the door standing open,' said the comte, 'so that we will all be in full view of any servants. Or summon your maid, Miss North.'

'I will leave the door open,' said Jane, won-dering whether she had imagined the whole thing. 'I was looking down from the window a moment before and I saw a man with his face mostly covered in a closed carriage op-posite. He ... he was levelling a pistol at you.'

'Really?' said Jamie, thinking that Miss North was every bit as tricky as Frances.

But for a moment, the comte's usually lazy eyes were sharp and shrewd. 'Which one of us did he aim to kill?' he asked.

'I do not know,' said Jane wretchedly. 'I now think I must have imagined it all. And yet ... and yet when I called to you, he shouted to his coachman and sped off.'

'Odd,' said Jamie, his eyes dancing. 'But London is full of footpads.'

But the comte, covertly studying Jane's pallor, was thinking of a meeting he had had earlier at Horse Guards where he had been told of a certain letter from the Duke of Rowcester in which the duke had explained some conspirator he believed to be an English gentleman was out to kill the Comte de Mornay. At Horse Guards, they knew that the comte's spying activities against Napoleon had in the past been a thorn in the side of the emperor's friends and supporters. They had urged him to use caution but at the same time to try to find out the name of this English traitor.

'Did you notice anything about the carriage, Miss North?' he asked. 'Any crest, any distinctive hammer-cloth? Surely the coachman was not masked?'

'It was just a plain carriage,' said Jane, 'and the coachman just looked like any other coachman.'

'No groom, footman or tiger on the backstrap? No livery?'

Jane shook her head.

Jamie gave a light laugh. 'We will watch very carefully how we go in future, Miss North. Our meetings seem destined to be dramatic.

Firstly, poor Miss Haggard here faints nearly at our feet in Curzon Street and now you are on hand to prevent us being murdered.'

Jane looked at him haughtily. 'I did not make the whole thing up. Now, since your presence here is highly unconventional, gentlemen, I suggest you take your leave.'

But at that moment Harriet came in, followed by her maid, her eyes darting from one to the other. 'Explain,' she demanded curtly.

So Jane explained again, conscious all the time of the amusement in Mr Ferguson's eyes. Her story began to sound ridiculous in her own ears.

'How odd,' said Harriet coldly. 'Now, pray take your leave, gentlemen. You should not be here. We will no doubt see you at the Farleys' ball.'

'That will be our pleasure,' said the comte. With elaborate bows, both men made their farewells.

'Minx,' laughed Jamie as soon as they were clear of the house. 'How inventive! How cunning! And how flattering. Are you not flattered that such a beauty should tell such lies to catch your attention?'

'She had had a bad shock, my insensitive friend, or did her unusual pallor escape you?'

Jamie stopped short. 'You cannot mean

she was telling the truth!'

'Trust me, mon ami. The beautiful Miss North really believed she saw a man with a gun.'

'Why would anyone want to kill one of us?'

But the comte had no intention of explaining anything. 'London is full of villains and footpads,' he said, tossing a coin to a diminutive crossing-sweeper.

Harriet had retired to write to her husband, and Jane and Frances were once more left alone. 'So you did not make it up?' asked Frances, her eyes round.

Jane shook her head in bewilderment. 'I really believe I saw a man with a gun. But in broad daylight and in Park Street! I feel so ashamed of myself. I must have imagined the whole thing. And your Mr Ferguson thought I had planned the whole thing to get their attention.'

'And so you did. No, I do not mean you lied. But you did get their attention, and now we know they are going to be at the ball.' Frances pirouetted about the room. Then she sank down next to Jane in a flurry of taffeta. 'But she will no doubt be there, Fiona Dunwilde, and I shall have to watch him making sheep's eyes at her. Tell me she will have changed, Jane. She is quite old now and the Scottish climate is reported to be harsh. The Scotch drink a great deal of claret and spirits, and so she may have a red nose and broken veins on her face.'

'We will know when we see her,' said Jane absent-mindedly, thinking all the time of that masked face at the window of the coach.

In their private sitting room that evening, the hoteliers gathered to discuss their future plans, the main one being that they were to organize and arrange the serving of the supper at Lady Farley's ball.

'I do not see why we should not tell Harriet we are going to be there,' complained Miss Tonks.

'She has much on her mind,' said Lady Fortescue. 'She is doing us a favour by bringing Jane out. We do not want her mind distracted by wondering in advance how to cope with her old friends acting the role of servants.'

'We ain't servants,' grumbled Sir Philip. 'We've engaged servants to do the work. It's Despard's famous cuisine Lady Farley is after.'

'But we ourselves have to appear to serve,' explained Lady Fortescue patiently. 'It is part of our cachet.'

'Cachet be damned,' growled Sir Philip. 'It's time we got back in society and took up our rightful places.'

'Which we could do,' said the colonel eagerly, 'if we were to sell this hotel.'

'Society isn't quite going to forget we were once in trade,' said Lady Fortescue.

'If you've got money,' said Sir Philip cynically, 'society will cheerfully forget everything.'

'Then why isn't Almack's full of Cits?' asked Mr Davy.

'Because Cits never were in our class to start with.' Sir Philip glared at him. 'They're all common ... like you.'

'That will be enough of that.' Miss Tonks bridled. 'Let us change the subject. I gather our prince is not to be present at the ball.'

'He was asked but he don't want to go,' said Sir Philip. 'He uses this hotel like a small palace. He likes his own people about him. Lady Farley could have had him if she had invited his whole retinue. He never moves without 'em. How's Harriet?'

'The duchess sent a note by hand this morning,' said Lady Fortescue, 'to say that the duke had written her a wonderful letter. She says she will be so pleased to see him that she plans to wear some barbaric family necklace he is so proud of for the first time so that he will see her decorated with it on his return.'

Sir Philip felt quite cold with fear. He knew all at once that the necklace to which Harriet had referred was the one in the glass case in the muniments room at the duke's country home, the one he had thieved to raise money to start the hotel and replaced with a clever replica. Nestling as it was now in the dim light of the muniments room, the fake was safe from detection. But he had a sudden vivid little picture of a radiant Harriet wearing it and the duke smiling, taking out his quizzing-glass, and then beginning to shout he had been tricked.

'Think I'll stretch my legs,' he said, getting to his feet. Out in Bond Street, he hailed a hack and told the driver to take him to Holborn, upon which the driver promptly demanded payment in advance for venturing into an area which bordered on the Rookeries, those slums so full of crime and vice. Normally Sir Philip would have cursed and haggled but he was too worried to argue and settled for the fee of a shilling.

It seemed to take an age to get to Holborn but at last he was deposited outside the shop – or where the jeweller's shop used to be. He climbed stiffly down, calling sharply to the driver to wait. A sign above the door said 'Welsh Bakery.' Although the shutters were up, he could see chinks of light from inside the shop streaming through. He rapped furiously on the door with the silver knob of his stick and fretted and fumed as slow shuffling feet could be heard approaching from within. Bolts were drawn back, the door was opened a few inches, the end of a blunderbuss pointed at him, and a hoarse voice said, 'Who's there?'

'Where is the jeweller?' demanded Sir Philip, who had no intention of giving his name.

The door opened farther, revealing the baker himself, a small, squat, powerful man dusted with flour. 'Gone,' he said, 'two months since, and nothing but the constable and people like yourself a-hammering and trying to find him. The Runners have been round as well. Arsk at Bow Street.'

The door was slammed in Sir Philip's face. He stood irresolute on the greasy pavement, until the driver hailed him with 'I ain't going to wait about here all night.' Sir Philip climbed back into the smelly hack and asked to be taken back to Bond Street, his thoughts in a turmoil. The villainous jeweller had decamped and with him his stock and along with his stock that necklace which Sir Philip had been going to reclaim, and along with it all the money Sir Philip had been paying him in instalments to buy it back. Sir Philip decided to wait until daylight and then question his underworld contacts for news of the jeweller.

But although he searched and searched on the following day among the narrow streets and stews of London, no one had heard anything about the jeweller. Only the fact that he had to return to the hotel and change and go to Lady Farley's to take up his duties made him give up his frantic search.

Harriet was more like the débutante than Jane herself, reflected Jane as they set out for the ball. The duchess looked radiant, her green eyes sparkling like the emeralds about her neck. Beside her, Jane felt diminished, sad, and underneath it all she had a niggling feeling of dread that someone at the ball would recognize her. The only thing that gave her courage as they approached the large mansion in Grosvenor Square was a determination to do her best to shine to please her generous hostess and to try to help Frances with her romance. Frances,

Jane knew, envied her, Jane's, looks. And yet Jane envied Frances her happy nature, her confidence, even her mad plans to secure the man of her dreams.

Lady Farley's town house was imposing, with a line of liveried footmen on either side of the red Turkey carpet leading up to the front door, but Jane's home was imposing as well, the earl liking to entertain with great ceremony, and so she did not feel intimidated.

They left their wraps with their maids in the ante-room off the front hall and together they mounted the staircase to the 'ballroom' on the first floor, which was in fact made out of a chain of large saloons, with most of the furniture removed for the occasion. Lady Farley, a widow, stood at the top of the stairs with her son, the Honourable Clarence Farley, to receive the guests. She murmured a few gracious words and then Harriet and Jane walked into the main saloon, which was draped in gold silk and set about with banks of hothouse flowers. Frances came up with her mother to greet them and introduced Jane to her father. Jane had not until that moment met Mr Haggard. He was an older, masculine version of his daughter, his frizzy hair pomaded and powdered, and he had the same twinkling eyes and childlike air of geniality.

Frances drew Jane aside. 'She is here!' she whispered.

'Lady Dunwilde?'

'The same.'

'Which is she?'

'There. Dancing with that colonel.'

Jane looked covertly over her fan. Lady Dunwilde was a striking matron with auburn hair and eyes so dark grey, they looked black. She had a voluptuous figure shown to advantage in damped muslin. Beyond her, Jane noticed Mr Jamie Ferguson leaning against a pillar and staring intensely at the love of his life.

'Only see how he looks at her,' hissed Frances. 'We have our work cut out. This dance is over. Oh, pray someone asks me. I do not think I could bear to sit against the wall all evening, an object of pity. But if no one asks me, that is what I shall have to do. Be still, my heart, and fan me ye winds! Here comes your comte with my beloved. Smile!'

But Jane looked at the approaching comte with the same pleasure with which she would have observed an approaching snake. He was formidably handsome at the best of times, but in all the glory of evening dress and jewels, he seemed to eclipse every other man in the room. He bowed before Jane and said, 'Miss North, will you do me the very great honour of allowing me to lead you in a set of the quadrille?'

Jane curtsied low and said she would be delighted, although, the comte reflected wryly, she looked anything but happy.

They were joined in their set by Frances and Jamie. Jane noticed that Jamie was saying something in a low voice to Frances, and then how Frances's eyes flew to Lady Dunwilde and how she nodded. So they are going on with their plan, thought Jane. Frances is to make a confidante of Lady Dunwilde.

The comte, who had addressed her twice, asking if this were her first London ball, looked down at her, amused at his own sharp feeling of pique. He was used to ladies hanging on his every word. 'And only remark how Lady Farley has just slit her throat,' he said.

'Yes, indeed,' replied the preoccupied Jane politely, having become aware at the last moment that she was being addressed.

The music began and the couples twisted and turned in the intricate measure of the dance, which did not allow for any opportunity for conversation. Frances danced with great expertise and elegance, Jamie noticed, thinking indulgently that she was indeed full of surprises. When the dance was over, they promenaded in the round, as was the custom. Jamie contrived to come alongside Lady Dunwilde and her partner. He bowed low. 'Lady Dunwilde, may I present Miss Haggard; Miss Haggard, Lady Dunwilde.' Frances curtsied and then said, 'I am delighted to meet you, Lady Dunwilde. You are even more beautiful than I had been led to believe.'

Oh, silly little Miss Haggard, thought Jamie. No one could be pleased with such a blatantly insincere compliment. But to his surprise Lady Dunwilde smiled graciously and patted Frances's cheek. 'Dear child,' she murmured. 'Come and chat with me.'

With every evidence of gratified delight, Frances trotted off at Lady Dunwilde's side. They sat down against a bank of flowers on those uncomfortable seats called rout-chairs. 'Tell me,' said Lady Dunwilde, fanning herself languidly, 'have you been long acquainted with Mr Ferguson?'

'For about perhaps a little over a month,' said Frances, omitting the fact that apart from the day before, she had seen nothing of Mr Ferguson, despite her efforts, during that month.

Lady Dunwilde turned those very dark

eyes of hers on Frances. 'You must not have hopes in that direction, my child.'

'Why not, my lady?'

She sighed. 'He was much in love with me before I married Lord Dunwilde ... and he still is. Alas, an undying passion, I fear.'

'It seems a pity that such devotion cannot be rewarded,' said Frances.

Lady Dunwilde's lips curved in a thin smile. The fan slowly moved. 'Oh, perhaps he may yet get his reward.'

Frances quickly raised her own fan to hide the sudden flash of dislike in her eyes. 'Where is Lord Dunwilde?'

'At home at present, although he will join me later. He is a martyr to the gout. But you must go and join the young ladies, and do tell Mr Ferguson that there is always hope.'

Frances rose and curtsied and gave Lady Dunwilde her best smile. 'Of course, my lady. Always at your service.'

'Do you know, I have taken quite a fancy to you, dear child. I shall call on you.'

'I am honoured and flattered, my lady.'

The fan flicked in a dismissive manner.

As Frances skirted the floor, she met Mr Ferguson just as that gentleman was bearing down on Lady Dunwilde. 'What did she say?' he asked eagerly. 'Did she speak of me?'

'Yes.' Frances stared down at her little kid shoes.

'What did she say?'

'You had better ask me to dance and I will tell you.'

'But it is the waltz and ... and I wanted to ask Lady Dunwilde.'

'Oh, no, I would not do that, sir. I think you should hear what I have to say first.'

'Very well.'

He swept her onto the floor. Frances followed his steps, as lightly as a feather. He bent his head over hers. 'Now tell me.'

'Mmmm?' murmured Frances dreamily.

'Tell me what she said.'

Frances rallied. 'Lady Dunwilde asked me how long I had known you and I said over a month, which is quite true, don't you know. She said you had been madly in love with her.'

'Oh, my heart! And what did she say then?'

Frances looked up and met his eyes steadily. 'Lady Dunwilde said she had made the right decision in marrying Lord Dunwilde. She said that she believed you to be still spoony about her and that was a sign of great weakness in a man, in her opinion.'

'The devil she did!'

'But Lady Dunwilde is quite a kind

134

matron, I think,' Frances said earnestly, 'and it is gracious in one of her years to befriend me.'

'You are to see her?'

'She is to call on me.'

They danced on in silence after that. When the dance was over, supper was announced. Jamie gloomily took Frances into supper. His friend, the comte, he noticed, was escorting Miss North.

The comte sat down next to Jane at one of the long tables, waited until she had been served with food and wine, and then said lightly, 'And you should be careful of that collection of spiders your duchess keeps in the attics. Some of them are, I believe, quite poisonous.'

Jane only heard the bit 'be careful' and assumed it was some caution about the dangers of the streets of London, for her worried mind slid away from what he was saying. There was a lady present who looked like one of her father's friends, a lady who kept sending curious little darting glances in her direction.

'And I am madly in love with you,' went on the comte. 'Will you marry me? I think we should deal very well together. Do you not think so?'

Worried and abstracted, Jane only heard his voice asking the latter question and said politely, 'Yes, I do agree.'

Those blue eyes of his flashed with humour. 'Good. That is settled. Will you tell the duchess I shall call on her tomorrow to ask permission to pay my respects? And, of course, I must call on your father and mother.'

'Mother? Father?' said Jane, coming out of her abstraction. 'What are you saying? My mother is dead.'

'Your father, then.'

'Why? Why are you talking about my father?'

'It is usual under the circumstances. Since we are to be married, I should seek his permission.'

Jane upset her glass of wine. A waiter darted forward to mop up the mess and pour her another.

Now he had her full attention. Her eyes were magnificent, he thought appreciatively. 'Marriage? What marriage? What are you talking about?'

'I asked you to marry me and you accepted, very sweetly, too,' he said, all mock patience.

She coloured to the roots of her hair. 'I

know you are funning, Monsieur le Comte. I was abstracted. Worried. Thinking of other things. I thought I was replying innocuously to polite questions.'

'So you are not going to marry me?'

'No. I mean, definitely no. I would not sound so harsh if I did not know you were bamming me.'

'Perhaps. But what do you have against my suit? I am rich, unmarried, good *ton*.'

'I am not used to London ways or London gentlemen, Monsieur le Comte. Some other lady, most other ladies, would probably be considerably flattered by your attentions.'

'Where is your home?'

'Durbyshire.'

'Do you know the earl?'

'No!' Sharply.

'Why so vehement, Miss North?'

'I ... I have heard of this earl and do not like what I have heard. May we talk of other things?'

'Gladly. Do eat something. You will offend your friends from the Poor Relation if you do not.'

Jane looked across with surprise. She had been too abstracted to notice the presence of Sir Philip, Lady Fortescue, Colonel Sandhurst, Miss Tonks, and Mr Davy, but there they all were in various parts of the room, supervising the waiters, occasionally and graciously inclining to remove a plate or dirty glass with bejewelled hands.

'I hope nothing has gone wrong,' Jane heard the comte remark. 'That horrible old Sir Philip looks as if he is about to have an apoplexy.'

And Sir Philip felt so himself. For round the neck of Lady Farley lay a barbaric necklace he knew only too well. Somehow that perfidious jeweller must have sold it. What if Harriet knew that there could only be one like that? His heart was hammering with fear. Somehow he had to get that necklace from Lady Farley and replace it with the fake and put the real necklace back in the duke's muniments room.

When the supper was over he approached Harriet, who was being squired by an elderly military gentleman. 'A word with you, Your Grace,' he said and then glared at Harriet's escort, who was staring down his nose at him as if wondering at the sheer impertinence of these hoteliers.

Harriet murmured her excuses to her escort and walked off with Sir Philip. 'I just wanted to be sure you were enjoying yourself,' began Sir Philip.

'Yes, I thank you. I heard nothing but praise for Despard's cooking.'

'Know Lady Farley well, do you?'

'As much as one knows anyone in society.'

'Funny old necklace she's got on.'

'I remarked it,' said Harriet, 'because my husband has one like it at home. He wants me to wear it, although I do not like it much. I think he will be surprised to learn it is not unique.'

'I don't think anything is these days,' said Sir Philip. 'But it wouldn't surprise me to learn that Lady Farley's necklace is paste.'

Harriet laughed. 'You are the expert on such things. It looks very real to me. Jane appears to have some little animation this evening. Everyone is remarking on her beauty.'

'But you'll need to stop that comte from hanging about her,' said Sir Philip.

Harriet looked over his shoulder to the ballroom. 'Jane is dancing with Clarence Farley and getting on splendidly, by the looks of it. I shall endeavour to keep her away from the comte.'

Jane was enjoying the company of Clarence Farley. He was a serious man with a calm, courteous air. She felt safe with him in a way she did not feel at all safe with the handsome comte with his glinting blue eyes. When

Clarence suggested she sit out the next dance with him she readily agreed. They talked of innocuous things such as the weather and balls and parties to come. Clarence had thick brown hair and a not very memorable face, small brown eyes and a rather large mouth, but he was well dressed and seemed very much at ease in her company.

'How long have you known de Mornay? he suddenly asked.

'Not very long,' said Jane. 'And not very well.'

'You are new to London, Miss North. I feel I should warn you that de Mornay has the reputation of being an adventurer.'

For some obscure reason Jane could not fathom, she felt slightly annoyed at hearing the comte criticized. 'He is accounted well-to-go,' she said defensively.

'I did not mean adventurer in the sense that he pursues heiresses,' said Clarence. 'Only that he is flighty and breaks hearts.'

'My heart is quite safe, sir,' said Jane in a cold voice.

'Ah, now, Miss North, I would not offend you for the world. I feel we might be friends. May I ask Her Grace's permission to take you driving?'

'By all means.' Jane suddenly liked him

again. 'When?'

'You will be receiving callers tomorrow, myself included. Shall we say the day after that?'

'Delighted.'

'The next dance is about to begin and here come your courtiers. Until then, Miss North.'

Jane, performing the cotillion with her next partner, was pleased to see Frances was on the floor. In fact, Frances had not been left sitting out once since her conversation with Lady Dunwilde. It was, thought Jane, because of her ebullience and friendliness. Little Frances would be engaged to be married before any of the belles.

Frances smiled and talked to her partners, prattling away as if she did not have a care in the world, when all the time she was aware of Jamie. He had not approached Lady Dunwilde. And then, just as the dance was finishing, she became aware of him edging around the ballroom floor in the direction of Lady Dunwilde. She suddenly could not bear it. What if he found out so soon that she, Frances, had lied to him about what Lady Dunwilde had said?

Just as Jamie had nearly reached his quarry, Frances pretended to turn her ankle and let out a piercing shriek and swayed dizzily. Her partner, a shy young man, stared at her helplessly. Jamie, with a mutter of annoyance, ran to Frances's side and caught her in his arms.

'My stupid ankle,' whispered Frances, tears starting to her eyes, because all the feelings she had for him welled up in her and overset her senses. She could feel his arms around her, smell the light scent he wore, feel the heat from his body.

'There now,' he said. 'Lean on me. Where is your mother? I fear your dancing is finished for the evening.'

He had quite forgotten Lady Dunwilde for the moment. Frances was a silly child and needed someone to look after her. Jane came up, full of concern. She had thought Frances was pretending to twist her ankle but became alarmed at the strain on her face. 'I will find your mother, Frances,' said Jane, 'and then I think your parents should take you home.'

'I would like to sit quietly and perhaps drink a glass of lemonade,' said Frances.

'I'll fetch it for you,' said Jamie. When he returned with the lemonade, he noticed that Lady Dunwilde had been joined by her elderly husband. She cast a languishing look in Jamie's direction, but he was still smarting from what he believed to be her cruel remark to Frances, and so he turned away and bent solicitously over Frances with the lemonade and then sat down beside her, so that when Mrs Haggard came hurrying up, it was to find a radiant daughter who said that she was quite recovered and would sit quietly with Mr Ferguson. Mrs Haggard was so pleased with her daughter's unexpected success at the ball, for she had expected her to be totally extinguished by such dazzling beauties as Jane North, that she smiled indulgently on her and said they would take her home when she wished to go.

'I am so sorry,' said Frances to Jamie when they were alone. 'You must join your beloved.'

'I have no intention, Miss Minx, of joining my – as you call her – beloved. Her husband has arrived.'

'Do you mean to say she settled for that old man when she might have had *you?*' Frances's eyes over her fan were large and melting.

He laughed. 'You restore my amour propre, which has been sadly damaged. Why do you tap your little foot to the music? I thought that was the injured one.'

'It is,' said Frances quickly. 'It is when I

stand on it that it hurts. Do you want me to convey any message to Lady Dunwilde for you when she calls?'

'I should hate her,' he said gloomily. 'But, in truth, you may tell her that I still love her with all my heart.' The light went out of Frances's face and she said sadly, 'My foot hurts rather a lot after all. I would like to go home.'

She looked around to say her goodbyes to Jane, but Jane was waltzing with the Comte de Mornay. Despite her misery, Frances could not help noticing that Jane was smiling at something the comte was saying to her while Clarence Farley leaned against a pillar and watched them both closely. There was something in Clarence's look that Frances did not like, but she put it to the back of her mind. When Lady Dunwilde called on her, she should tell her the truth, that Mr Jamie Ferguson was still in love with her. Frances's lips set in a firm line. She had no intention of doing what she ought to do and she was suddenly determined to lie and lie until all hope was gone.

SIX

Marriage is a step so grave and decisive that it attracts light-headed, variable men by its very awfulness.

ROBERT LOUIS STEVENSON

The comte, being barbered by his valet the following day, roused himself from thought. 'You know I trust you, Gerrard?'

'As you have every reason to do, Monsieur le Comte.'

'I wish to send you on a mission of some delicacy.'

'Do you mean we return to France, milor?'

'No, I shall not be going. I wish you to travel to Durbyshire and find out what you can about a certain Miss Jane North who is being sponsored here by the Duchess of Rowcester. She is unforthcoming about her background and is quite vehement about the fact that she does *not* know the Earl of Durbyshire. I suggest you start with the earl's household. If he has a secretary, seek the man out. It will be he who knows all the

145

ladies of the county who are invited to balls and parties. Do we know an artist?'

'There is a certain gentleman of some little talent known to my brother Lucas.'

'Find him today. Miss North is of outstanding beauty. She has black glossy hair and large grey eyes fringed with heavy lashes. He is to position himself outside the Duchess of Rowcester's town house in Park Street, wait until the lady emerges, and do a lightning sketch. She will probably go out this evening, and it is light quite late. He must give the sketch to you and then you may take my travelling carriage and go north.'

'Yes, milor. An affair of the heart?'

'An affair of the curiosity, mon vieux!'

Jane awoke as Frances bounced into her bedchamber. 'What brings you here so early, Frances?' she asked, struggling up against the pillows.

Frances perched on the end of the bed. 'I have done a wicked thing and it is on my conscience.'

'Then you had better tell me.'

Jane listened wide-eyed as Frances told of her lies of the evening before.

'But Frances,' she exclaimed, 'sooner or later they will meet and will find out you have lied and both will despise you!'

'I don't care about *her* despising me,' said Frances, taking off her straw bonnet and swinging it by its satin ribbons. 'She is determined to be my friend because she wants my Mr Ferguson as her lover. So immoral! Such women should be hung, drawn, and quartered, and whipped at the cart's tail.'

'All at once, Frances? Now, be sensible. The next time she gives you a message for Mr Ferguson, or he for her, tell the truth and then forget about Mr Ferguson. You were in demand last night. You should be at home preparing for your gentlemen callers.'

It was the custom for gentlemen to call on the ladies they had danced with the night before, although some merely sent a card with a servant.

'I am sure Mr Ferguson will call on me.' Frances pouted. 'And all to give me further messages for his lady-love. But what of you and Mr Clarence Farley? Solid, dependable, although I do think, dear Jane, your rakish comte puts all others quite in the shade.'

'Even Mr Ferguson?'

'With the exception of Mr Ferguson. You are so sad and serious, Jane, perhaps a rattle is just what you need. Still, I suppose everyone has warned you about him.'

'Nearly everyone, I think, including Mr Farley, who is, by the way, to take me driving tomorrow.'

'Do be careful. There is something about Mr Farley I cannot like.'

'He seems a kind and sensible man,' said Jane wistfully. 'Just the type of man I always imagined would make a good husband.'

'My nerves were overwrought last night,' said Frances, 'so I am probably mistaken about him. Now I am so tired, for I did not sleep well because of an uneasy conscience, don't you know.'

'So you will not lie again?'

Frances got off the bed and tied on her bonnet. 'I probably shall, dear Jane, but perhaps I should not feel guilty about it. I am protecting Lady Dunwilde from committing adultery, after all!'

That same morning, Lady Fortescue summoned Mr Davy to her bedchamber. 'I am sorry to disturb you so early,' she said as he entered wearing a dressing gown and nightcap. 'I need your help. Jack, the footman, came to me to say he had a message from Limmer's that Sir Philip is there and imbibing freely. It is bad for a man of his years to start the day drinking so early. Pray go and

148

see if you can make him desist and get him to bed.'

Mr Davy held Lady Fortescue in high esteem, which is why he did not protest, for he would dearly have liked to refuse. He went gloomily back to his room and shaved and dressed and then made his way to Limmer's Hotel.

Sir Philip was in the coffee room glaring morosely at a half-empty bottle of wine.

His pale eyes focused on Mr Davy and he remarked, 'Why are you inflicting your presence of me, son of a whore, you bag of shite, you scum from the kennels?'

'I would gladly leave you to rot,' said Mr Davy amiably, 'were not Lady Fortescue concerned for your welfare. As a matter of interest, what drives you to the bottle at this early hour?'

Sober, Sir Philip would not have dreamt of telling him, but worry, drink, and a sleepless night had loosened his tongue. He had studied the doors and windows of Lady Farley's mansion before he had left and knew there was no way an elderly gentleman could play burglar and get through the many bolts and locks on the doors and windows. He felt everything was lost, and shame and exposure would result.

149

He made to pour another glass of wine but Mr Davy reached forward and caught hold of his hand. 'Drink coffee,' he urged. 'I might be able to help you.'

'You!' declared Sir Philip in accents of loathing. But he allowed Mr Davy to order a pot of coffee. All at once he had an urge to tell this actor his troubles, motivated by the knowledge that Mr Davy was not a gentleman and therefore would have no right to express shock or moral outrage had he belonged to that exclusive breed.

Mr Davy maintained a sympathetic silence until Sir Philip had drunk two cups of coffee. Then he said, 'Go on. What's it all about?'

So Sir Philip, in a flat, slightly slurred voice, told him all about the theft of the necklace to found the hotel, and its subsequent appearance on Lady Farley's neck, ending up with a moan of 'And how can an old man like me expect to broach the locks and bars of Lady Farley's house?'

'As to that,' said Mr Davy, 'I could help you.'

'You?' said Sir Philip contemptuously. 'How?'

'I still have many friends among the acting profession. Society is much given to amateur theatricals and like to employ people versed in the craft to show them how to go on. Were it to be suggested to Lady Farley that a little theatrical soiree would be just the thing, and you know the man to arrange it, then I can fix things so that you will be there. Once indoors, when all are watching the play, you should have an opportunity to slide away. I have noticed at these events that the servants are allowed to watch as well. You should be able to get to my lady's bedchamber un-observed. But in order to arrange this for you, I expect something in return.'

'How much?' sneered Sir Philip.

'No money. I simply want your promise that you will not interfere in my friendship with Miss Tonks.'

Sobering rapidly, Sir Philip studied him, his brain beginning to work quickly. Say yes, promise anything, he thought. He could propose to Miss Tonks himself after it was all over, and claim that was hardly interfering in their friendship; he hoped they would still be friends, yes, all that. And call on Harriet and try to steal one of her seals and copy her handwriting, for he would need a letter, sup-posedly to have come from her, giving per-mission to take that fake necklace to London, ostensibly for cleaning. The duke's servants had met him when he had called on a visit before.

'Very well,' said Sir Philip. 'You have my promise. I must go to the country and get that necklace. Do you think you can have all arranged for the play by the time I return?'

'Yes,' said Mr Davy, rising to his feet. 'You must accompany me back to the hotel to put Lady Fortescue's mind at rest.'

'Do not tell the others any of this,' said Sir Philip.

'You have my word.' Mr Davy looked at him curiously. 'But I do not understand why you never did tell them. They must have known it was something of extreme value to raise the necessary sum to get the hotel started.'

'They would have been too afraid,' said Sir Philip as they walked together out of Limmer's. 'It all seemed like a joke then. Harriet was not yet married to Rowcester, and he seemed then like such a pompous idiot ... well, I thought he deserved it. Then I let time slip by and slip by, and the longer time went by, the harder it seemed to tell any of them of what I had done.' He raised his cane and hailed a hack. 'Tell Lady Fortescue I am well. I must call on Harriet.'

Harriet was in her private sitting room when Sir Philip was announced. She looked at him half-annoyed, half-amused. 'It is an odd time to call, Sir Philip,' said Harriet. 'I am preparing to receive our callers, the gentlemen who danced with Jane and myself at the ball.'

Sir Philip's pale eyes turned thoughtfully in the direction of the little escritoire in the corner of the room. He must distract Harriet's attention. He could not pretend to suddenly feel faint, for she would simply ring the bell and summon her servants to help. He walked over to the window and looked down into the street. 'I am concerned about Jane,' he said. 'I do not think she should be encouraging the attentions of that comte.'

'Jane is not at all interested in the Comte de Mornay,' replied Harriet. 'Why! What is the matter?'

For Sir Philip had let out a stifled exclamation and was peering down into the street.

'Nothing,' he said hurriedly.

'There must be something.' Harriet went to the window. Sir Philip backed away. Harriet looked down but could only see a footman walking a dog. Sir Philip darted to that escritoire and pocketed a seal, a half-finished letter and a blank sheet of crested paper and thrust them both into his pocket just as Harriet turned round.

'I thought I saw an old friend,' said Sir Philip airily. Harriet looked at the old man suspiciously. 'Sir Philip, now I have assured you that Jane is well and not in danger of being seduced by the comte, is there anything else you wish to know?'

'Nothing, nothing,' said Sir Philip, backing to the door.

After he had gone, Harriet rang for her maid. 'Open the window,' she commanded. 'The room is airless.' The maid opened the window and a brisk breeze blew in and scattered the papers on Harriet's desk. The maid picked them up and put them under a paperweight. And later, Harriet, unable to find the letter she had started to write to her husband, assumed it must have blown away.

Jane, although she had had a rigid social training from Miss Stamp, found herself hard put to remember the names of the gentlemen who called that afternoon, with the exceptions of Mr Farley and the comte. The comte only stayed for ten minutes and was polite, courteous, and rather distant. She felt she should be relieved. Instead she found herself irritated with him and decided that his was the behaviour of a mountebank, proposing marriage to her one minute and ignoring her the next. And yet, despite that irritation, she often thought in wonder about her attempt at suicide. Day after day, there seemed to be so much to live for – Frances's friendship, the kindness of Harriet, the odd feeling of stability given by the knowledge that those hotel proprietors who had saved her life were still interested in her well-being, for Harriet told her that they always asked how she was getting along.

Pique at the comte's behaviour made her be very charming to Mr Farley, a fact that Harriet noticed with approval, although she would not have liked the reason for it.

When Jane left that evening for the opera with Harriet, Harriet said with some amusement, 'You really are London's latest beauty. A man across the road was sketching you!'

Jane flushed slightly. 'I never thought myself anything out of the common way.'

Harriet laughed. 'That is part of your charm. You are a sensible girl. I was glad to see you treat the comte with a certain amount of coolness.'

Jane, who had thought until then that she had behaved in no particularly remarkable manner towards him, began to wish she had not been so cold. Rake he might be, but the comte, apart from teasing her with that mock proposal, had been courteous.

'Although,' Harriet was going on, 'it will do your consequence no harm if he is seen to be paying attention to you. Since I am now sure your heart is in no danger from that direction, I think I may allow him to take you driving. Mr Farley, of course, is an excellent suitor. So sensible!'

So dull, said a little voice in Jane's head. So very dull.

Frances was at the opera in an adjoining box to Harriet's. Lady Dunwilde paid her a visit at the first interval and drew her aside. 'Did you give Mr Ferguson my message?'

'Yes, my lady.'

'And what was his reply?'

'It was most odd,' said Frances. 'He just laughed.'

'Ah, he laughed with pleasure.'

'Well, no, it was a sort of mocking laugh, and then he said, "Too late."'

Lady Dunwilde bridled. 'Then you may tell him from me that I have no feelings for him whatsoever.'

'Would it not be better just to ignore him, my lady? Someone as beautiful and charming as yourself does not need to waste time on a heartless young man.'

'He is the same age as I!'

'For sure, for sure. As you wish. I shall tell him.'

'Do that, and I shall call on you tomorrow to hear his answer.'

'But I may not see him.'

'He is just arrived in the box opposite, with the Comte de Mornay.'

Frances looked across the lighted theatre and saw Mr Jamie Ferguson watching them avidly. He did not look at all like a man who had been put off the love of his life with lies. She felt very young and silly. Here she was being used by this harpy to set up an adulterous affair. And if Mr Ferguson was the type of man to want an adulterous affair, then she did not want to have anything to do with him. Lady Dunwilde left. Other young men crowded into the box and Frances forced herself to sparkle and flirt and did it to such good effect that the comte, levelling his quizzing-glass across the theatre, said to Jamie, 'Miss Haggard is in looks tonight. She is a fetching little creature.'

But Jamie only saw Frances as a conduit for his hopes and desires. The performance was beginning again. He would need to content himself until the next interval to find out what it was that Lady Dunwilde had said.

But at the next interval, he could not get near Frances. Her box was full of callers and she made no effort to speak to him alone. He would need to wait until the ball after the opera.

The comte was finding a similar difficulty in getting near Jane when he visited Harriet's box. Mr Farley was there and the comte heard that tiresome man remind Jane of their engagement to go driving on the following day. He was surprised to find himself experiencing a bitter, sour feeling which, after some quick thought, he identified, to his surprise, as jealousy. He slipped out of the box and summoned one of the opera foot-men and told him to go into the Duchess of Rowcester's box and tell Mr Farley his mother wished his company immediately. He waited until he saw Mr Farley leave, then re-entered the box and sat down quickly next to Jane.

'Alone at last,' he said.

'That is because the performance is about to begin,' said Jane.

'It is?' He settled himself more comfortably in his chair. 'Too fatiguing to return to my own box. I shall stay here.' Jane looked to Harriet for help, but Harriet's eyes were fixed on the stage. Jane was barely aware of the last act, only of the handsome figure next to her, aware that his eyes were often fixed on her face. Her breathing began to become rapid and shallow and she was relieved when at last the performance was over. But it seemed the comte was going to accompany them through to the ball, offering an arm to each and smiling all around in a sort of proprietorial way.

Harriet, noticing all the little envious glances cast in their direction, decided to indulge the comte. In Jane's averted glance, Harriet only read that Jane did not particularly care for the comte and decided it would be safe to use his escort to bolster Jane's standing in society. It did a lady no harm to be seen to be courted by a rich rake, provided that lady was well-chaperoned.

For her part, Frances knew the moment had come when she had to put an end to the lies. So when Jamie immediately approached her and asked permission to take her to the floor for a waltz, she sadly agreed. 'I have a confession to make,' she murmured. He bent his head and smiled indulgently, 'What have you been up to?'

'Telling lies,' said Frances.

'Bad lies?'

'Very bad.'

'Do you want to tell me?'

'I must. Lady Dunwilde did not say any of those cruel things. She wishes to have an affair with you.'

His face darkened. 'What? What is it you say?'

'I was to tell you there was still hope.'

'Why did you lie to me? Why?'

'I do not approve of adultery. I do not like Lady Dunwilde.'

She raised her eyes to his but he was looking across the room to where Lady Dunwilde was dancing and his face was suddenly radiant. 'I am sorry,' whispered Frances.

'Eh? Oh, all forgiven, I assure you.'

At the end of the dance, after the promenade, he escaped after surrendering Frances up to her next partner. As she was led off, Frances watched him cross the floor to claim Lady Dunwilde's hand for the dance, saw the quick exchange, saw the baleful look Lady Dunwilde cast in her direction, and tried to persuade herself she had done the right thing. Despite her distress, she noticed that Jane appeared to be enjoying the comte's company. They were sitting out, drinking lemonade, and Jane did not seem to be aware that Clarence Farley was glowering at them from behind a pillar.

'So although you tease me about my rakish disposition, Miss North,' the comte was saying, 'I am glad you can tease me about something. Do you think rakes can ever reform?'

'I am not well enough up in the ways of the world,' said Jane, 'but no, I do not think so. You are a sad flirt.'

'On the contrary, at the moment I am a very happy flirt. Tell me why you have honoured Farley with your company.'

'He is...'

'Safe?'

She gave a reluctant laugh and he was pleased to hear that laugh.

'Yes, safe. Talk about something else.'

'Let us observe Miss Frances. Smitten as I am by your charms, I remarked that Miss Frances talked very seriously to my friend Mr Ferguson during the waltz. Mr Ferguson looks startled, angry, then elated. Your little friend looks cast down, although she is putting a brave face on it. Off goes Mr Ferguson to Lady Dunwilde's side.'

'I do not know,' said Jane loyally, although she was sure that Frances must have told

Mr Ferguson the truth.

'You even lie prettily. Another forbidden subject. So let us return to you. Do you have brothers and sisters?'

'Four brothers in the military,' said Jane.

'And are you fond of them?'

'I barely know them. I was born when they were grown men. My mother did not live for very long after I was born.'

'So you were raised by your father. Who is your father?

'Mr North,' said Jane, opening and shutting her fan nervously.

'And Mr North is a landowner?'

'Yes, Monsieur le Comte.'

'How large is his property?'

'I do not know. How large is your property, sir?'

'I do not own land ... yet. I was brought to this country by my parents after the Terror. They brought a quantity of jewels with them but settled down in an undistinguished suburb to eke out their remaining days by selling one jewel after another. I became interested in stocks and shares, a genteel form of gambling. I took the remaining jewels and was able to make a fortune for myself and them, so that their final days were passed in comfort. I keep thinking of the family lands in

Burgundy. Perhaps they will be restored to me. Perhaps I may go back there one day. But I have a mind to buy myself a property in England. Perhaps in Durbyshire? What do you think, Miss North?'

'I have no views on the matter.'

He smiled at her, his blue eyes glinting in that mocking way which disturbed her so much. 'I can see it now – a pleasant mansion, some rolling acres, and children tumbling about the place. In my mind's eye, it is always sunny. I shall return from inspecting my property and she will be there to meet me with the children gathered about her skirts.'

'Monsieur le Comte,' said Jane with a slight edge to her voice, 'you are a romantic. I am persuaded that your wife will be entertaining her friends while the children are abovestairs in the schoolroom being bullied by some ferocious governess.'

'Which is what happened to you, Miss North?'

'We were not discussing me.'

'True. But think again of my picture, Miss North. Do you yourself not have dreams? Do you not imagine having your own establishment with a loving husband? Close your eyes. Cannot you hear the laughter of the children and the sound of the wind in the trees?'

Jane thought of her grim childhood, and to her dismay a tear rolled down her cheek.

'Now what have I done?' asked the comte. 'I would not distress you for the world. Pray tell me what ails you, Miss North. Your servant, your devoted slave, ma'am.' The laughter had left his eyes. There was only kindness and concern.

Jane pulled herself together with a great effort, for that kindness in his eyes evoked in her a strong temptation to lean on him, to tell him everything, to ask for his help. But perhaps that was all part of the comte's lethal charm.

Clarence Farley bowed before her. 'Our dance, Miss North.'

She rose to her feet and curtsied. The comte rose at the same time and bowed and then went off in search of Harriet.

Harriet was talking to Mrs Haggard. 'Duchess, may I have your permission to take Miss North driving?'

Harriet looked up at him, thinking again how handsome he was. She thought quickly. It was only a drive in the Park. Jane could not come to any harm. She appeared to be getting on so well with Clarence Farley. That interest would keep her safe. And it would do no harm to give Mr Farley a little competition. 'Miss North is engaged to go driving tomorrow,' she said. 'Perhaps the day after? At five?'

'Delighted,' said the comte.

Mrs Haggard watched him go. 'Are you sure that was wise?'

'Oh, I think so,' replied Harriet. 'I have made extensive inquiries about this comte. He does not have a reputation for seducing virgins. He is amusing himself with London's latest beauty. To change the subject, Frances is quite a success.'

'Yes,' agreed Mrs Haggard complacently. 'We had many callers today. I am no longer worried about her prospects.' But she looked up in surprise as Frances came up to her at the end of the dance and said hesitantly, 'Would you mind very much, Mama, if I were to return with Jane after the ball?'

'I do not see why,' said Mrs Haggard rather crossly. 'It is Her Grace to whom you should be addressing your request.'

Harriet, seeing the pain at the back of Frances's eyes, said quickly, 'You know what it is like. They want to discuss beaux. Of course you are welcome, Frances. And there is no need for a footman to bring your night-rail, for I can supply you with anything that is necessary, and one of Jane's gowns will serve you for the morning.'

Mrs Haggard opened her mouth to protest and then closed it. A duchess was a duchess, and it would do Frances's consequence no harm to be seen on such free and easy terms with the Duchess of Rowcester and her protegée.

So, at the end of the ball, an uncharacteristically silent Frances travelled home with Harriet and Jane. Jane was not surprised when Frances appeared in her bedchamber after she had courteously said goodnight to Harriet, crying, 'I must tell you all. It is all too dreadful.'

Jane listened sympathetically while Frances told her about revealing the truth to Mr Ferguson, ending up with a wail of 'And he was too happy to reprimand me!'

'I think you really must forget about him, Frances,' said Jane. 'You cannot still have any feelings for a man who is even contemplating an affair with a married woman.'

'It is the fault of that friend of his, that comte,' said Frances mulishly. 'Just because that frivolous Frenchman finds it amusing to court married ladies, there is no reason for Mr Ferguson to do the same. Do you think he can be reformed by the love of a good woman?'

'Meaning yourself?' Jane looked at her sadly. 'I do not think so. From my observation, the ladies of society marry for convenience and then fall in love afterwards, and not with their husbands.'

'But the Duchess of Rowcester is so in love with her husband, and he with her. Everyone talks of it.'

'There are exceptions, Frances, but it is not usual, or so I believe.'

'What of love? What of romance? Would you settle for someone like Clarence Farley?'

'Yes, I can see that I might. It would mean freedom of a kind, an establishment of my own, children.' A little smile curved Jane's lips and she said dreamily, 'Rolling acres and a tidy mansion and the children at my skirts when he rode home.' For a moment she saw herself on a summer's evening standing outside such a house, but the man on horseback coming down the drive was the comte, not Mr Farley. She blinked the bright dream away.

The comte, after having said goodnight to Mr Ferguson, waited in vain for his carriage to be brought round, finding after quite half an hour that someone had told his coachman to go home, that he intended to walk.

He set off through the dark streets in his evening finery, wondering what his valet would find out about Jane, marvelling the whole time that his mind hardly ever strayed away from her.

So absorbed was he in his thoughts that he almost did not hear the pounding of feet after him until it was too late. As it was, he swung around, drawing his dress-sword, and swerved to the side at the same time, just missing a murderous blow from a cudgel. With his back to the wall of a building, he faced his assailants, for there were three of them. They tried to rush him but his sword flickered like lightning, piercing the man with the cudgel in the arm and then sweeping round to dart at the other two, who fell back, turned round and took to their heels. The man with the wounded arm was stumbling off. The comte caught him, swung him round and held the point of his sword to his throat.

'What were you after, mon brave?' he asked.

'Your jewels, money, that's all. I swear.'

The point of the comte's sword pressed a little harder into the man's neck. 'Try again. Who sent you?'

'No one, yer honour,' gasped the man.

The comte thrust him away in disgust. 'Faugh, you smell abominably.' But his assailant, finding himself released, suddenly took to his heels and ran away with surprising speed, down a dark alley to his left. The comte debated whether to follow him but thought the man's friends might be waiting. He could not believe the attack was an accident. Someone had sent his coach away. Someone had wanted him to walk home.

Someone had wanted him dead.

SEVEN

I feel the pangs of disappointed love.
NICHOLAS ROWE

Two weeks had passed since Lady Farley's ball and Sir Philip and Mr Davy were closeted in the hotel office.

'You have the necklace?' asked Mr Davy.

'Yes, they handed it over with no trouble at all,' said Sir Philip. 'Now what about this play? I put the idea in Lady Farley's head before I left.'

'It is Act Two of *The Beaux Stratagem*. We have a few professional actors, including myself, but Lady Bountiful is played by Lady Farley. You play the part of one of the stagecoach passengers at Boniface's inn. But as soon as Scene Two has been underway for a couple of minutes, you rise and exit. They will think you are playing the part of a departing passenger.' Mr Davy took out a roll of paper and spread it out on the desk between them. 'Here is a plan of the house which I have sketched for you. Here is my lady's bedchamber. If she plans to wear the necklace in the play, I will dissuade her and say it is not suitable for a Restoration comedy. You must make your way to her bedchamber by the back stairs. The servants are to be present at the play, standing behind the guests. Lady Farley wants as big an audience as possible for her talents.'

'Can she act?'

'Not in the slightest. She seemed surprised that she actually had to learn lines and could not command a servant to do it for her. But that is not your affair. I have had to endure such performances before.'

'What do you play?'

'Gibbet, the highwayman.'

'What if her jewel box is locked?'

'Sir Philip, unless I am not mistaken, you are perfectly capable of springing the simple lock usually found on jewel boxes.'

'Maybe. And when is this to take place?'

'This evening.'

'This evening!' echoed Sir Philip in alarm. 'Good God, man, what if I had not yet returned!'

'You sent an express to Lady Fortescue saying exactly when you were to return. It all worked out beautifully. You will not forget your promise?'

'No, no,' said Sir Philip testily. 'I shall not interfere with your friendship with Miss Tonks. Thinking of marrying her, hey?'

'I did not say that.'

Good, thought Sir Philip, then I shall propose, and I can say in all innocence that you talked only of friendship.

'What if it does not work?' he asked aloud, biting his knuckles nervously.

'Provided you are quick and deft, it should work.'

'That son of hers, Clarence; I don't want him snooping around'

'He plays Aimwell. He fancies himself as another Kean.'

'Then it should work,' said Sir Philip. 'You have not told any of the others?'

'Of course not. You have my word.'

For what that's worth, thought Sir Philip nastily.

'I am becoming increasingly concerned about Sir Philip,' said Lady Fortescue to Colonel Sandhurst and Miss Tonks later that day. 'He is nervous and jumpy. He disappeared to the country and refused to tell us where he was going. I hope he isn't putting our money on horses.'

'He can't,' said the colonel. 'I keep tight

172

control of the money, and Miss Tonks here does the accounting.'

'We are become so wealthy,' said Miss Tonks wistfully. 'Do we sell when our prince leaves, or not?'

The colonel held his breath.

'I think we might,' said Lady Fortescue.

A look of sheer gladness lit up the elderly colonel's face.

But Lady Fortescue's next words wiped it away. 'I thought,' she said in a considering way, 'that as we have all dealt so extremely well together, that we could all share a house in Town and begin to entertain.'

Colonel Sandhurst's happy picture of a trim manor in the country, shared with his bride, Lady Fortescue, whirled about his head and vanished.

Miss Tonks did not know what to think. Before the advent of Mr Davy she would have been delighted at the prospect of company for her declining years, but now she felt afraid. The magic title of 'Mrs' seemed as far away as ever. What if Mr Davy used his share of the money to launch some theatrical venture? The colonel, Lady Fortescue, and Sir Philip were all so very old that they might soon die and she would be left alone again. Mr Davy was pleasant and courteous to her at all times; in fact, he went out of his way to seek her company. But how could a man who had spent his life surrounded by beautiful actresses contemplate marriage to a faded spinster in her forties?

Also, Mr Davy had joined Sir Philip immediately on his return, and they had been closeted in the office. There was something conspiratorial about them. Besides, Mr Davy had organized a theatrical event at Lady Farley's, but when Miss Tonks had hinted shyly that she would like to go with him and be of help, he had not seemed to hear her.

She saw the pain on the colonel's face. She knew the colonel wanted to marry Lady Fortescue and so decided to leave him alone with Lady Fortescue while she herself tried to find out what Mr Davy was up to with Sir Philip.

When Miss Tonks had left the room, the colonel cleared his throat. He was about to remind Lady Fortescue of her promise to consider his offer of marriage and that they should retire together to the country, but all at once he found he could not. He dreaded an outright rejection. Lady Fortescue was talking about menus and the possibility of getting new curtains for all the rooms and the colonel took that to be a sign that she did not mean to sell up at all, for what was the point in refurbishing a place they were about to leave?

That evening Sir Philip, in the costume of a stagecoach passenger, which meant wearing his own clothes and having his elderly face smeared with nasty greasepaint, stayed on the stage for a whole two minutes before looking at his watch with a well-feigned start and taking his leave. He made his way to the back stairs with ease, having studied the map Mr Davy had drawn for him. As Mr Davy had predicted, most of the servants appeared to be at the back of the audience. He climbed to the upper floors, and consulting his map again by the light of an oil lamp in one of the passages, located Lady Farley's apartment. With a sigh of relief he looked around. He walked through her sitting room to her bedroom. The jewel box lay on the toilet-table, a large brass-bound affair. He took out his penknife and examined the lock.

Downstairs, Mr Davy saw trouble. Lady Farley, who had been like the worst prima donna during rehearsals, had considered the applause for her performance in the first scene of the Second Act not sufficient. To his horror, he saw her get up and stalk off in a sulk, followed by her maid. There was no way he could rush and warn Sir Philip.

Upstairs, Sir Philip had sprung the lock on the jewel box. With a smile of triumph, he took out the real necklace and substituted the fake. To his even greater relief, the lock proved undamaged and he was able to close the box again. There would be no signs of burglary. He was just making for the door when he heard Lady Farley's voice, high and petulant 'I gave a fine performance, Clorinda, did I not?' and the maid's answering, 'Yes, indeed, my lady. You rivalled Siddons.'

'Then why did not they give me the applause I deserved?'

Sir Philip dived under the bed. He lay there sweating with fear while Lady Farley complained that her nerves were overset and she would retire early and that no one appreciated her, all punctuated by the sycophantic compliments of the maid.

Let her go to sleep, please let her go to sleep, prayed Sir Philip. He heard the maid retire. He heard the body on the bed above him turn and twist, searching for a comfortable position. And then his nose tickled. He grabbed it to stifle the sneeze he felt rising. In the treacherous way of sneezes, it appeared to subside, but the minute he released hold of his nose, the sneeze erupted.

He heard Lady Farley's cry of alarm. There was only one thing to be done. He shot out from under the bed, whipped back the bedcurtain, and cried, 'Do not betray me. I did all for love.'

In the light of a candle on the bedtable, Lady Farley shrank back against the pillows and stared up at Sir Philip's face, where the greasepaint had melted as he sweated with fear and was running in streaks.

'Do not cry out, beloved,' he panted. 'I love, you!' Had he left it at that, then Lady Farley, whose hand was already reaching for the bell-rope, would have screamed for help, but fear had inspired Sir Philip. 'It was your performance, my lady,' he gabbled. 'Magnificent. I have never seen anything like it. You stole my poor old heart away.'

The fear and outrage vanished from Lady Farley's face and she actually simpered. 'Why, Sir Philip. You old rogue!'

'I cannot help it,' said Sir Philip, striking his bosom. 'I am ever susceptible to beauty. I had to see you alone, to tell you how I adore you. Now, having told you of my love, pray let me retire and leave you to your slumbers.'

What an awful woman she looked, he thought, with her skin ruined by too many years of application of white lead and her hair thinned by dyeing.

She gave him a flirtatious smile. 'Do you know, Sir Philip,' she said, 'I think such love should receive its reward, do not you?'

'I could not dare to hope for any favour,' cried Sir Philip in genuine anguish.

'Silly man. Come here.'

And just before he did what he had to do, Sir Philip thought of his colleagues with real hatred. The things he did for them!

The following day, Mr Jamie Ferguson prepared to meet his love. Lord Dunwilde was to be in the House of Lords that afternoon to make an important speech. Lady Dunwilde had told him that she had given the servants the afternoon off. The road to adultery lay straight before him. He was just adjusting his cravat when the comte was ushered in.

'Good day,' said the comte, subsiding gracefully into a chair. 'I came to suggest you accompany me. I am to take Miss North driving. I have been deliberately cold in that direction so as not to alarm her or her protectoress. But Farley sees more and more of

178

her at ball and party, the safe, so dull Farley. If you came with me, perhaps we could take up little Miss Frances. Then Miss North would relax more in my company.'

'Alas, my friend, I am bound for Lady Dunwilde's.'

'Oho, and his lordship is known to be giving an important speech in the House – or rather, important only to the old bore himself. So you are about to have your heart's desire? Eh, bien, I shall nonetheless call on Miss Frances first and see if she is free and allowed to come with such an old rake as myself, although come to think of it, she is so extremely popular that I shall probably find she is engaged.'

'Miss Haggard popular!'

'My dear Jamie, because she lied to you about what your soon-to-be mistress told her and you have been so studiously avoiding her, you must not yet have noticed that she never sits out a dance. She is a prime favourite.'

'To be sure, she has a certain charm.'

'She will make some man a good wife. All that liveliness and warmth and honesty. I shall leave you to your fate. Or rather, I can set you down at Lady Dunwilde's on my way there.'

Jamie glanced at the clock and gave a reluctant laugh. 'If I go now, I shall be too early and may meet his lordship on the doorstep. I tell you what, I shall call on Miss Frances with you. It is silly to bear a grudge against one so young and heedless.'

'Splendid. Let us go.'

To Jamie's surprise, Mrs Haggard's drawing room appeared to be full of gentlemen callers. To the comte's request to take Frances with him while he drove Jane, Mrs Haggard said, 'I am afraid, as you can see, Frances has too many people to entertain this afternoon. Perhaps another time.'

A footman carried around a tray with wine and cakes. Jamie helped himself to a glass of wine. He had come to talk to Frances and so he felt he may as well stay until he did. He still had plenty of time. Besides, Fiona Dunwilde had been cruel to him, damned cruel, and so she deserved to be made to wait a little. And now she is being damned cruel to her husband, said a voice in his head. He did not take her away from you by trickery or guile. She went gladly.

He joined the little court of men around Frances who were looking at her sketches. Somehow, by dint of inserting himself in front of her admirers, he managed to isolate her from them until they were left briefly alone.

'Forgiven me yet?' asked Frances in her usual direct way.

He smiled. 'Of course.'

Her face brightened. 'Why, then we can be comfortable again.'

He laughed. 'I could forgive the world this day. I am on my way to see Lady Dunwilde.'

Her expressive face became a mask of distaste and she said primly, 'Do not let me detain you. Ah, Mr Samson, you are lurking in the background and you will quite break my heart if you do not admire my sketches.'

A young man bounded eagerly forward. He was, Jamie guessed, only about a year or two older than Frances. He had an engaging smile and a mop of carefully coiffed blond curls. Jamie moved away. He heard Frances say something and heard this Mr Samson laugh.

All at once he felt rather grubby, and what had appeared to him earlier like a rapturous adventure seemed now in his eyes just to be another sordid society intrigue. The comte would not be troubled by conscience, he thought, looking across at his handsome friend. But the comte, he realized with a little shock, despite his reputation, had never really

181

hurt anyone. The ladies were either widows or racy matrons with philandering husbands who did not give a rap what their wives got up to, provided it did not appear in the windows of the print-shops or the daily newspapers. His feet felt like lead as he walked to the door. He looked back. Little Frances was once more surrounded by her admirers. She appeared to have forgotten his very existence. She looked young and happy and innocent.

'Are you coming?' asked the comte at his elbow. 'We have stayed our regulation ten minutes.'

'Yes, yes, I suppose so,' said Jamie fretfully. They made their goodbyes and walked together out to the comte's carriage.

The comte climbed in and took the reins. His tiger jumped on the back. 'Come along, mon ami,' said the comte lightly. 'I will leave you at your lady-love.'

'I will walk, thank you,' said Jamie abruptly. The comte gave a Gallic shrug and drove off. As he turned the corner of the street, he twisted his head and looked back. Jamie was still standing there, his hat in his hand, looking up at the house.

Harriet walked into Jane's bedroom just as

the maid was putting the finishing touches to Jane's hair. 'You have such a busy calendar these days that I cannot keep pace with your engagements,' said Harriet. 'Mr Farley again?'

'You forget, Harriet,' said Jane. 'The Comte de Mornay is to take me driving.'

'I suppose I must trust him to behave,' said Harriet doubtfully. 'I have been glad to see that he regards you with a certain indifference, Jane.'

And Jane should have been glad of that as well, instead of remembering all the times she had danced with Mr Farley conscious the whole time of the tall, handsome Frenchman moving about the ballroom.

'I am going to settle down and read a letter from my husband,' Harriet went on. 'I have been saving it for a quiet moment.'

They walked down to the drawing room together just as the comte was announced. Harriet was struck again by his looks and thought that he and Jane made a handsome couple. It was a pity their characters were so unsuited.

'I called to see if Miss Haggard would care to join us but found her surrounded by admiring gentlemen,' said the comte as he handed Jane up into his carriage. 'I am lucky to find you not similarly besieged.'

'The duchess sometimes refuses callers when she wishes a quiet day,' said Jane. 'She has received a letter from her husband which she has been treasuring so that she may read it when she is alone.'

They drove off in the direction of the Park in the comte's phaeton, his horses stepping out proudly. The day was fine and warm. Jane was wearing a broad-brimmed straw hat with lilac silk ribbons, a lilac silk gown embroidered with lilac flowers, and around her shoulders she wore a handsome Norfolk shawl. She looked around at the Fashionables strolling on the pavements and once more wondered how long this holiday, this respite from the agonies of home, would last. She had received a letter from her old nurse confirming that her letters had been sent on to her father and that he had not replied to any of them. But the day would soon come when his pride would not suffer a stubborn daughter and then he would go in search of her. When that day occurred, she had told her old nurse to tell her father the truth, that she was in London, or her father might take out his anger on the nurse.

The comte, glancing sideways at her, thought that the light and shade of different emotions chased across her face like cloud shadows over the countryside.

'So how are you enjoying the Season?' he asked, as he turned his carriage in at the gates of the Park.

'Very well, I thank you,' said Jane politely.

'Rumour has it you are to marry Mr Farley.'

'Indeed? Society is full of rumours.'

'He is not for you. He has a bad temper and would beat you.'

'Mr Farley? You are funning. He is all that is amiable.'

'I have warned you, Miss North. I do not think you know him very well. I have made certain inquiries and do not like what I have heard.'

'Would you like me to believe the rumours that I hear of you?' asked Jane, tilting her lilac silk parasol so that she could see his face. 'That you are a heartless philanderer?'

'I *was* a trifle flighty,' he said easily. 'But how I have changed! I am sedate and boring and highly respectable. Have you noticed me paying any particular attention to any female this Season?'

'I do not know, sir. I have not remarked your behaviour particularly.'

'Alas, all my good motives gone for nothing! You are heartless, Miss North.'

'Not I,' retorted Jane with a reluctant laugh.

'When you laugh like that with that beautiful mouth of yours, I feel like kissing you.'

'Monsieur le Comte!'

'Why not? Do you not think of me even a little, Miss Jane North? Do you never wonder what it would be like to feel my lips against your own?'

'If you are determined to continue in this strain; then I suggest you take me home.'

'Home being?'

'Why, Harriet's – the duchess. Where else?'

'I mean your home. You never said where it was.'

'Durbyshire.'

'Exactly where?'

The parasol tilted to hide her face. 'Oh, look,' said Jane, 'there is Mrs Barber.' The comte bowed in Mrs Barber's direction and Jane nodded. Mrs Barber, who barely knew either of them and whom Jane had only recognized as one of Mrs Haggard's friends who had been pointed out to her at a party, looked gratified.

Now they were among the throng of Fashionables and so were too busy nodding and bowing to make conversation. Jane began to relax. They would make the round a couple of times and then the comte would take her home and she could settle down again to contemplate the idea of marriage to Mr Farley. He was on the point of proposing, of that she was sure. All she had to do on the road home was to parry the comte's questions. Nothing out of the way would happen.

Harriet had been enjoying her husband's letter. He was on his way home and would shortly be in Paris. Paris! Her eyes glowed. He said that by the time his letter reached her, he might even be at the coast, finding a ship to Dover. The servants would meet him at Dover and he planned to drive to London as fast as possible. She relished every affectionate phrase. There was still pain over the loss of her child, but now sheer gladness as well that the estrangement between herself and her husband was over. And then she got to the end of the letter.

'*I did not tell you of an intriguing adventure on the road to Milan,*' the duke had written.

I was at an inn and overheard conspirators plotting the release of Napoleon. This, my dear, is nothing out of the common way, as many who gained power and influence under that monster's reign of terror wish their positions back. But one of them was English, I will swear, and they were planning to kill a certain Comte de Mornay who has, it appears, been instrumental in foiling other plots. A friend in Milan before I left told me that Mornay was in London. I wrote to Horse Guards telling them to warn him. And now, my beloved wife...

Harriet put down the letter. Jane was driving with the comte and someone was trying to kill the comte and that put Jane in danger. She called for her maid and changed into a carriage dress and sent a footman with an urgent note to the Poor Relation calling for help, never for a moment in her distress thinking that it would have been more sensible to call out the Runners than to send to such elderly people as the colonel, Sir Philip, and Lady Fortescue for help. Then, with her coachman driving, she set out for the Park herself.

The hoteliers felt they could not wait to order a carriage from the livery stables, and with Sir Philip, exhausted and shaky after his adventure of the night before, complaining loudly that this is what came of being too mean to own a carriage of their own, they hailed a smelly hack and howled to the driver to take them to the Park.

But when they got to the Park, they were stopped by a ranger who was not going to let a battered hack anywhere near the fashionable throng and so they had to get out and walk, with Sir Philip stumbling after them over the grass, clutching his side and moaning he was not long for this world.

The comte, unaware of all these people rushing to his rescue, reached the end of the second round and regretfully decided he must obey the dictates of fashion and take Jane home.

And then a shot rang out, a loud report, and he felt the wind of a ball as it whined past his face. His horses reared and plunged in fright and then took off across the grass, with Jane screaming and clinging to the rail. To Jane the Park passed her in a blur of frightened staring faces from carriages and trees and bushes. Shouting and swearing in French, the comte eventually controlled his maddened horses, hanging on to the reins, letting out a slow breath of relief when they finally slowed. He had left his tiger behind that day, so first he jumped down and ran to their heads, patting and soothing them, until the quietened horses began to crop the grass.

Then he returned to Jane. He lifted her

gently in his arms down from the carriage and set her on the grass. He looked solemnly down into her white face and said gently, 'We are safe now.'

'That was a shot,' cried Jane. 'Someone was trying to kill us!'

'Me, I think. How white you are. You need colour. Even your beautiful lips are white.' He bent his head and kissed her on the mouth, and Jane, too overset, as she told herself later, to push him away, clung to his shoulders and let his mouth caress hers in a long, lingering kiss.

The comte at last freed her mouth and smiled down at her dreamily. 'Would that an assassination attempt happen to me every day so that I might claim such a reward.' He turned his head and looked across the Park. 'Good heavens, here comes your patroness, looking like thunder, and with those hoteliers.'

Harriet had taken up the hoteliers who, unlike Harriet, had not stopped to change into appropriate dress. Miss Tonks was wearing a morning gown and lace cap, the colonel certainly was as correct as usual, as was Lady Fortescue, but Sir Philip was in his dressing gown and nightcap and Mr Davy in his shirt-sleeves.

'We are safe,' said the comte, hoping Harriet had not witnessed that kiss.

'What happened?' demanded Harriet. 'People were shouting about a shot.'

'Someone shot at me,' said the comte pleasantly, as if, thought Jane, someone trying to kill you were an everyday occurrence. 'Why are you all here?'

'The Park rangers are coming,' said Harriet. 'I received a letter from my husband in which he said he had overheard a plot in an inn near Milan to kill you. I will take Jane home with me and perhaps when you have dealt with affairs here you may join us, Monsieur le Comte, and tell us about it. Jane, come with me.'

Jane, overset with conflicting emotions, felt that she should tell Harriet about that kiss, but at the same time she hoped Harriet had not seen anything, or she would forbid Jane to see the comte again. Not that it was important that she see the comte again, for she was surely going to marry the bad-tempered Mr Farley, was she not? Jane felt quite dizzy with all these thoughts. She was squeezed into Harriet's carriage beside the hoteliers.

As she was driven out of the Park, she saw Mr Farley standing up in his carriage and staring at her. Oh, heavens, he would call to see how she was. But if she was even considering marrying the man, she should not be, oh, dear, dismayed at the thought of his breaking into what, now the shock was receding, seemed like an exciting adventure.

She replied to the others' eager questions. All she knew, said Jane, was that there had been the sound of a shot which had narrowly missed the comte; his horses had bolted, but fortunately neither of them had come to any harm.

And then Harriet said, 'It would be as well, dear Jane, to keep clear of this comte in future if he is going to be the target for some assassin.'

'That seems too hard,' protested Jane. 'He needs our help, surely.'

'We will see what he has to say,' said Harriet. 'I think we could all do with a refreshing dish of tea.'

'Brandy, more like,' muttered Sir Philip. He was feeling old and tired and he knew he must set out for the duke's country home on the following day to return the real necklace to its case.

They had been seated a few minutes in Harriet's pleasant drawing room when Clarence Farley was announced. It was a day of surprises. Jane said hurriedly, 'I am too overset to see him. Pray say we are not at home.'

And so Clarence, looking every bit as angry as the comte had claimed he was, stomped off. But he waited outside in his carriage and had the doubtful pleasure of seeing the Comte de Mornay arrive and be admitted. He waited all the same, expecting the comte to reappear shortly, having been given the same message as himself, but as the minutes dragged on he realized to his increased fury that the comte was a welcome guest where he himself was not.

The news of the attempt on the comte's life spread through the West End like lightning. Frances and her mother received the news very quickly, for Mrs Barber had just been about to leave the Park when the assassination attempt happened. She had driven straight to her friend, Mrs Haggard, to tell her the news.

'Poor Jane!' exclaimed Frances. 'Mama, I must have the carriage. I must call.'

'But Mrs Barber is just arrived.'

'I do not need you to come, Mama,' said Frances, already halfway out of the room, and without waiting to hear any protest from her mother she shouted down the stairs to the butler to have the carriage brought round and then called up the stairs to her maid to make ready to accompany her.

As she tripped out onto the pavement, she stopped in surprise. Jamie was standing there. He saw her and a rather sheepish smile crossed his face. Frances thought quickly. The other callers had left an hour ago. Either he had already visited Lady Dunwilde and returned, or he had been there all along.

He bowed low and said, 'It is late to go driving.'

'I am on my way to see Jane,' said Frances. 'Someone tried to kill your friend, the Comte de Mornay.'

'Good heavens! May I come with you?'

'I should be glad of your escort,' said Frances, wishing her maid were not with her, not to mention the coachman in front and the footman on the backstrap. She wanted to ask him about Lady Dunwilde, but could hardly ask him outright in front of the servants.

'What happened?' he demanded as the carriage moved off. She told him the little she knew and then said in a low voice, 'And how was your friend? Your *female* friend?'

'I am afraid I do not know,' he said. 'The

194

air was so pleasant outside your house that I felt rooted to the pavement and could not move.'

Her eyes were shining under the little brim of her saucy hat. 'You did not go?'

'No, Miss Frances, I did not.'

'Why?'

'Later,' he said. He did not quite know himself. Only that as he stood outside her house, he had felt that as long as he stood there he was safe from taking an action which might leave him feeling nothing but shame. He felt he had managed to hang on to his immortal soul, and then almost laughed out loud at that dramatic thought.

When they were both ushered into Harriet's drawing room, they stared in surprise at the hoteliers. Sir Philip, in his dressing gown and nightcap, was curled up in an armchair by the fireplace, fast asleep.

They listened to the comte's account of his adventure. 'But why should anyone want to kill you?' asked Frances.

'I may as well tell you now that I am retired, so to speak, from business,' said the comte. 'I proved myself useful to the British government as a spy. In the earlier years, before I knew my City ventures would become profitable, it gave me adventure and provided me with an adequate income.'

'So you are not just a dilettante! You are a brave man!' said Frances ingenuously. 'But what danger you are in! How can you protect yourself?'

'Things are not so black. I have a surprise for you. Just before you arrived, the authorities called here, for I told the Park rangers where I could be found. The culprit was seen.'

'Who is he? Some ruffian?' asked Harriet.

'No, it was young Freemantle.'

Jamie gasped. 'Not Jerry Freemantle?'

'The same.'

'But he is of good family!'

'Let us think about Mr Freemantle,' said the comte. 'Deep in debt and duns at the door, as everyone knows. Cut off by his family. Wild, heedless, and usually drunk. Suppose someone approached him with an offer of money to shoot me? It would look like a very easy way of making money. I do not think for moment that young Freemantle is a supporter of Napoleon. I think what is interesting is who paid him to try to kill me. The militia have gone to try to find him, and weakling that he is, I have no doubt he will talk, and then, dear Duchess, we will find the name of this Englishman your husband overheard. An Englishman who speaks fluent French is a rarity.'

'But we in society speak French the whole time,' exclaimed Jamie, who prided himself on his knowledge of that language.

'At the risk of hurting your feelings, mon ami, society appears, during the long wars with the French, to have developed a French language of its own which bears little resemblance to the original. I heard a young lady say the other day, "Donnez-moi ça dos," by which she meant, "Give me that back."'

'And what was up with that?' asked Jamie, puzzled.

The comte raised his eyes to heaven. Harriet's butler interrupted by saying that there were 'some persons' below who wished to speak to the comte.

'I shall return soon,' said the comte, 'and hopefully with the news that young Freemantle has been found and has revealed the name of the arch-conspirator.'

They waited anxiously while he went belowstairs. 'I do hope it will soon be over,' said Harriet, finally breaking the silence. She looked up as her butler came back into the room. 'A message from Mr Farley, my lady,' he said, handing her a note folded in the shape of a cocked hat. She read it carefully and then looked at Jane with a little wry smile on her lips. 'Mr Farley is to call on me tomorrow afternoon to discuss a matter of some importance. You are, if I am not mistaken, to receive your first proposal, Jane.'

'A most suitable choice, if I may say so,' said Lady Fortescue. 'Quiet, stable, and worthy.'

'Eh, what?' demanded Sir Philip, who had woken up.

'I was commenting on the glad news that it appears Mr Clarence Farley is to apply for her hand in marriage of our Jane.'

'What's glad about it?' grumbled Sir Philip.

'He is surely a most suitable catch,' said Miss Tonks.

'Don't like him.' Sir Philip blinked sleepily about him. 'When we were catering at the ball, a little maid dropped a glass. It did not even break, but Farley snarled at her, reduced her to tears and then told her to leave his mother's employ.'

'Perhaps we are all forgetting that the decision to marry Mr Farley or not is Jane's,' said Mr Davy.

All eyes turned on Jane. She pleated the fringe of her shawl nervously between her fingers. 'I do not know Mr Farley very well,' she said at last.

'Then I would counsel you to ask for time rather than throw away a good prospect out of hand,' said Lady Fortescue. 'Yes, I think that would be best. Plead for a little time to get to know each other better. He cannot take offence at that.'

All eyes turned to the door as the comte re-entered, his face grim. 'Young Free-mantle hanged himself before they could get to him. This is a bad business.'

'Had he left no clues? No papers?' asked Jamie.

'Whatever he had, he had burned.'

'Then he must have had some loyalty to Napoleon after all,' exclaimed Jamie. 'Else why should he try to protect his fellow conspirators?'

The comte shrugged. 'Who knows? Per-haps he wanted only to protect other poor dupes like himself.'

'I do not want to appear too hard, Mon-sieur le Comte,' said Harriet. 'But as your life is in danger, it follows that anyone in your company is also putting their life in jeopardy. I must therefore suggest that Miss North should avoid your company for the present.'

'As you wish,' said the comte with seeming

indifference. Jane found she was bitterly hurt. After that kiss, he should have at least shown some regret. He was a heartless flirt. She found herself becoming extremely angry indeed. She would see Mr Farley tomorrow, and although she would not accept his proposal, she would follow Lady Fortescue's advice and not turn him down flat.

EIGHT

Talk'st thou to me of 'ifs'? Thou art a traitor: Off with his head!

SHAKESPEARE

Jane could see no sign of the angry man that the comte had warned her about as Clarence Farley, seriously and intensely, got down on one knee and asked her to marry him.

'Please rise, Mr Farley,' she said, 'and sit by me.' Many of her doubts about him had receded. He looked so solid and dependable, a rock in a shifting world.

'I am very flattered by your proposal. You do me great honour. I have decided to be honest with you. Firstly, I would like a little time to get to know you better. Secondly, I am not Miss Jane North.'

His eyes were sharp. 'Who are you?' he asked bluntly.

'I am Lady Jane Fremney, daughter of the Earl of Durbyshire.'

'But this is bewildering! Why the secrecy?'

In a low voice, Jane told him about how

201

and why she had run away from home. She did not tell him of her attempted suicide, something of which she was now bitterly ashamed. 'I must make it plain to you, sir,' she said earnestly, 'that even if we decide we do suit, then my father might not let me marry you and I will not have freedom to do so until my twenty-first birthday. I may have no dowry.'

His mind worked rapidly. His desire for her was waning fast. Because of the duchess's patronage, because of Jane's expensive clothes, he had expected a handsome dowry. He was all at once relieved that she had not accepted his proposal. On the other hand, he had a desire to spite the comte. It would also amuse him, he reflected, to send an express to the Earl of Durbyshire, telling him what his daughter was up to. In fact, he would do it as soon as he got home. Meanwhile he would pretend to want her despite her lack of dowry, and after hearing her story he was perfectly sure her father would not give her any.

He put his hand on his heart. 'Money means nothing to me. You are all I want. Pray say you will take tea with myself and my mother tomorrow. To get better acquainted, you should know my mother better.' And that would also keep his mother off his back, he thought sourly. She was always plaguing him to marry.

'I am honoured by your invitation and I accept,' said Jane. They both rose and he kissed her hands and bowed his way out.

Harriet entered almost as soon as he had gone. 'Did you accept him or tell him to wait?' she asked.

'I told him to wait,' said Jane. 'I also told him my true identity.'

'Oh, my dear, was that wise?'

'I warned him that I might not be able to marry him until I was twenty-one and that Papa might not give me a dowry and he said it did not matter. I am going to take tea with his mother tomorrow. I am ... I am pleased with him, Harriet.'

Harriet looked at her shrewdly. 'But not in love with him?'

'I do not know what love is,' said Jane. 'But I trust him and respect him and that is surely a better basis for marriage than any easy, fleeting feelings.' And I cannot forget the comte's lips against mine in the Park, she thought with silent anguish, or how easily he accepted the fact that he should not see me while his life was in danger.

Frances was announced. Her eyes were

sparkling and Harriet, guessing she had secrets to tell Jane, tactfully left the room.

'Mr Ferguson did not go to Lady Dunwilde yesterday,' said Frances breathlessly. 'He came here with me instead and he is to see me at the opera tonight. I am so happy I could cry.'

'I am happy for you.'

'And I have already received *two* proposals of marriage. Mama is in alt. I did not accept either, but it is very flattering to be in demand.'

'I, too, received a proposal of marriage today,' said Jane. 'Mr Farley.'

'Oh, dear.'

'Frances, you are incorrigible. He is all that is kind and good.'

'So you accepted him,' said Frances dismally.

'I told him to wait, that we should get to know each other better. And something else.' Jane told Frances of her real identity and Frances listened with avid interest to Jane's flight from home. To Frances it all seemed like some glorious Gothic romance. 'And you told Mr Farley all this? And he did not mind?'

'No, not in the slightest.'

'Well, to be sure, that was very noble of

him. I must readjust my mind, for I had quite decided that it was to be the brave comte after all.'

'The Comte de Mornay has no interest in me.'

'He always watches you, even when he is putting up an appearance of ignoring you. I noticed that,' said Frances. 'I think he has been playing a game, playing a game of being cool towards you to animate your interest and not frighten you away.'

'*I* think he is a hardened flirt,' retorted Jane sharply.

'He has that reputation. Has he flirted with you?'

The desire to confide was too much for Jane. 'When the horses bolted with us after someone tried to shoot him, after they had quietened, he lifted me down and he kissed me ... on the mouth.'

Frances heaved a sigh. 'Oh, that my Mr Ferguson would be so bold! Did you faint or slap his face?'

'Neither. I was too overcome. The shock, you see. But it meant nothing to him, for when Harriet told him that he should not see me so long as he was a target for an assassin, he accepted without a murmur.'

Frances looked at her doubtfully. 'A gentleman could hardly say anything else. And do you remember what Sir Philip said yesterday ... about Mr Farley's temper?'

'Sir Philip is always inclined to be waspish. I would guess that he would have encouraged me to go in any direction other than towards the comte.'

'I shall pray for you,' said Frances simply. 'I can see you are about to warn me not to tell anyone your secret and I shall not.'

The comte was reading a letter from his valet, Gerrard.

The Earl of Durbyshire employs a cook rather than a chef, and so I was able to ingratiate myself into her good graces, although she is like her kind, fat and bad-tempered and given to gin. I showed her the sketch and she cried out that it was a picture of Lady Jane Fremney, the earl's daughter. This Lady Jane is believed to be residing with her old nurse after having refused to marry one of the earl's elderly friends. Having learned what you wished, I changed the subject, claiming I was a London artist and that the sketch had been given to me by a fellow artist who must have taken the likeness when he was last in Durbyshire. The servants in general seem to hold this Lady Jane in great contempt for

some reason, and I gather that her former gover-
ness, now elevated to companion, a Miss Stamp,
is encouraged to treat her harshly.

The rest of the letter concerned the date of
the valet's return to London.

So that explained the sadness at the back of
her eyes, thought the comte, and then, with
French pragmatism, he came to the conclusion that it was as well he was a wealthy man,
for he doubted whether he could expect any
dowry. The fact that he was determined to
marry Lady Jane came first to him as a surprise, followed by tingling anticipation and
then relief. Damn this assassin. He must find
out who was at the back of the attempts on
his life, or he would not only have to fight this
earl for Jane's hand in marriage, but Harriet,
Duchess of Rowcester, as well.

Frances called the next day just before Jane
set out to the Farleys'. 'Such intrigue,' she
cried. 'I met the comte with my beloved at
the opera last night and could not but tell
him of Mr Farley's proposal to you. He
adopted an air of indifference, but I told
him how you had said that you both must
get to know each other better and that you
were going to take tea with Lady Farley at

207

four o'clock today. He stifled a yawn and drawled, "I hope she will be happy."'

'What else did you expect?' snapped Jane. 'That philanderer has no interest in me.'

'But I observed him when he thought I was not looking and his face was quite grim and set. I had not seen him look like that before. And he did not attend the ball but said goodnight and left at the second interval. Mr Ferguson, who knows him very well, said he looked very angry.'

'Pooh, it all means nothing to me,' said Jane, drawing on her gloves. 'I must go.'

Frances surveyed her anxiously. 'Do not be coerced into saying anything *definite*.'

'It is only tea, a brief visit.'

They walked down the stairs together. 'I mean,' persisted Frances, bobbing her head so that she could peer up under the brim of Jane's hat, 'do not let fear of your father drive you into an unsuitable marriage.'

'What my father planned for me was more unsuitable than you could possibly imagine, Frances. Do not worry about me. And I have something to tell you. I wager my best fan that Mr Ferguson will have asked for your hand in marriage by the end of the week.'

'If only that were true.' Frances looked rueful. 'He is so kind and friendly, but nothing of the lover there.'

'I am sure your efficient mama will have found a way to tell him of your two proposals of marriage. Harriet tells me that nothing spurs a man on like competition.'

'If that is true, your comte will be having quite a frightful time imagining you in the arms of Mr Farley.'

'What? Over the tea-tray?' Jane laughed and climbed into the carriage, which was waiting outside. 'Call on me tomorrow and I will tell you all about it.' She was driven off.

Frances climbed into her own open carriage. 'Home, miss?' asked the coachman.

'Yes, no, perhaps... Let me think.' Frances sat scowling horribly, until she realized that she was being surveyed by the comte and Mr Ferguson from the pavement.

'Oh!' said Frances, blushing. 'I was just thinking of you.'

'Which one?' asked Jamie.

'You,' said Frances, pointing at the comte with her parasol.

'Pleasant thoughts, I hope?'

'No, not at all. I think you are being very stupid,' said Frances, looking intently into the comte's blue eyes. 'Jane has gone to take tea with Lady Farley and her son. She has not yet accepted his proposal, but I fear he may press her. You kissed her and then ignored her, Monsieur le Comte, and no lady will ever forgive anything like that.'

The comte's face became a well-bred blank. 'Yes, I know I am being impertinent,' said Frances, 'and you may stare down your nose at me as much as you like. But you should go to the Farleys' yourself and tell her you want her for your wife before she does anything stupid.'

To Jamie's amazement, the comte swept a low bow, said, 'Certainly,' and strode off down the street.

'I do believe he is going to do what you told him to do,' said Jamie.

Frances smiled at him shyly. 'May I take you up? Are you going anywhere in particular?'

He felt light-hearted. Sun was drying the morning's rain from the pavements. He sprang into the carriage. 'Let us just drive around.'

A little smile of triumph curving her lips, Frances gave the orders to the coachman and settled back happily beside him.

Jane looked around the saloon of Lady Farley's home and said, 'Where is your mother, Mr Farley?'

'My mother had to rush off to see a sick friend. She sends her deepest apologies, but hopes to return in time to see you before you leave.'

Jane sat down on the very edge of a sofa, feeling nervous. Clarence had only spoken the truth. He had been annoyed at his mother's sudden departure, for all romantic feelings towards Jane had fled. The door of the saloon was wide open and servants came and went. Jane's maid was seated in the hall below. Despite his mother's absence, it was all very respectable.

The tea-tray was brought in with all the implements. Jane offered to make the tea, as it was the fashion for society ladies to make the precious brew rather than entrust the job to a servant. Clarence said he would prefer Indian tea, and so she opened up the lacquered teapot and selected the correct canister. While she worked away, Clarence experienced a certain pang of disappointment that she was dowry-less. He had sent an express the day before to the earl, so Jane would soon be removed from London and that would spite the comte. His eyes previously sharpened by jealousy, Clarence was well aware that the comte was fascinated by Jane. Now watching all that beauty bent over the tea-urn, he wondered whether it might not have been better perhaps to secure such a prize for himself, dowry or not. Although he had no longer any tender feelings for her, all men would admire and envy him. He knew that, in a day of dashing bucks and beaux, he was considered stodgy and dull.

The butler came in to say that there was a gentleman in the hall waiting to see him. Clarence studied the card, which had been proffered to him on a silver tray, and gave an exclamation of annoyance.

'Pray excuse me, Miss North,' he said. 'I shall only be a few minutes.'

Jane found that as soon as he had left the room, the very air seem to lighten. There was something threatening about Clarence Farley, almost oppressive.

She rose and walked to a low console table which held a few books: two bound volumes of the *Gentleman's Magazine,* one volume of the latest novel, no doubt Lady Farley's, and Foxe's *Book of Martyrs.* With a wry smile she picked up the *Book of Martyrs.* Miss Stamp delighted in reading aloud long passages of torture and death. Jane flicked back the cover and stared in surprise. The book was hollow. Inside was nothing but a small leather-bound notebook. Normally she would not have dreamt of looking through anyone else's private belongings, but the strangeness of the hiding-place caused her to open the notebook. There was a short list of names, with payments made to each in a neat column. She turned the pages. Always the same names, with regular payments. On the last page, one name had been scored through with a thin line, but she could still read that name – Gerald Freemantle. Gerald ... Jerry, the young man who had hanged himself!

She heard Clarence returning and slipped the notebook into her reticule and shut the fake *Book of Martyrs* but had not time to replace it exactly at the bottom of the pile of books, so she left it on the top and hoped he would not notice.

'A trifling matter of business,' he said. Jane sat down and began to dispense tea, proud in an odd way that her hands did not shake, for the import of those names was hitting her more and more. It could be innocent. They could be gambling debts and Jerry Freemantle's name was simply scored out because, being dead, he no longer needed to be paid. And yet she had taken that notebook and hidden it in her reticule and did not have the courage to question him about it. Her frightened thoughts turned to the comte. He would know what to do.

Her inner fear gave her an air of fragility which heightened her beauty. Clarence felt his senses quicken again. 'Have you considered my proposal?' he asked.

Jane forced herself to smile. 'It was only yesterday, Mr Farley. We are just starting to get to know each other.'

Mr Farley smiled back. 'Well, we shall see...' he began and then his wandering eyes came to rest on the console table, sharpened and remained fixed on it.

Then he turned his eyes back to Jane and studied her face and to her own horror she felt a guilty blush rising to her cheeks.

The butler entered. 'The Comte de Mornay,' he announced.

'We are not at home,' said Clarence, rising and going to the table. He picked up the *Book of Martyrs*.

'I would like to see the comte,' said Jane. She suddenly shouted, 'Monsieur le Comte. Here!'

There was the sound of a short altercation and then quick footsteps on the stairs and the comte entered just as Mr Farley opened the fake *Book of Martyrs* and saw that it was now empty.

'Shut the door, my lord,' he said. He

crossed to a desk against the wall, opened it and took out a pistol. He swung round and pointed it at Jane. 'You have an item which belongs to me. I assume it is in your reticule. No, do not move, Monsieur le Comte, or I will shoot her dead. Throw the notebook on the floor, Lady Jane.'

'So you know who she is,' said the comte.

'And now her father will know where she is because I sent him an express yesterday,' said Clarence.

The comte was leaning against the wall, inside the door, looking cool and amused.

Jane took out the notebook and tossed it down in front of him.

'What was in it, my sweeting?' asked the comte lazily.

'A list of names and payments,' whispered Jane, 'and one of them was Gerald Freemantle. His name had been scored out.'

'So you are a traitor, mon brave,' said the comte. 'But you have not been out of the country recently. But no doubt the gentleman who was plotting my death in an inn outside Milan has his name in your book. 'Why? Why work for a monster like Napoleon Bonaparte?'

'Because,' Clarence spat out, 'if he is restored he will not fail next time to invade

England and then the scum of society with their drinking and whoring will be hanging from the lamps in the street.'

'Dear me, all the young bloods who dub you Dreary Clarence? And to get revenge on them you would betray your country! Just what do you plan to do now? You can hardly shoot us both dead in a houseful of servants in the middle of fashionable London.'

The pistol levelled at Jane's heart never wavered. 'I will take her with me. So long as she keeps quiet, her life will be safe.'

'Tut, tut,' said the comte reprovingly. 'What makes you think that I would assist you in betraying my adopted country for the life of one poor wench?'

'Because you are in love with her,' sneered Clarence.

'Alas, you have the right of it.'

And I love you, too, thought Jane miserably. I have loved you all along, and now it is too late. This monster will never let me live.

'Move towards the door, Lady Jane,' said Farley, 'and do not make any sudden moves. Stand aside, Comte.'

Jane was moving slowly towards the door when it suddenly opened and Lady Farley swept into the room and walked directly between Jane and her son. She stared at the wicked-looking pistol in her son's hand. 'What are you doing, Clarence?' she screamed. In that moment, the comte moved forward, Jane darted behind him, and the comte clipped Lady Farley round the waist. 'Now what are you going to do, Farley?' he asked. 'Shoot your own mother?'

Lady Farley screamed hysterically and struggled in the comte's arms. Servants came running into the room. Clarence looked solemnly at all of them, put the pistol in his mouth and blew his brains out. The comte released Lady Farley, turned round and grabbed Jane and pressed her face into his breast, saying, 'Don't look, my love, my dear. It is all over.'

Harriet, fretting because Jane had not returned, decided to call on Mrs Haggard. Jane perhaps had gone straight from the Farleys' to call on Frances instead of coming home and getting ready to go out to the opera.

When she mounted the stairs to Mrs Haggard's drawing room it was to see Mr and Mrs Haggard outside the closed door with their ears pressed to the panels.

'What is the matter? Is Jane here?' asked Harriet.

'Shhh!' admonished Mrs Haggard. 'Mr Ferguson is proposing to Frances.'

'So you have not seen Miss North?'

'No! Shhh!'

Harriet, puzzled, turned away.

Inside the drawing room, Frances was being ruthlessly kissed by Jamie and feeling she would faint from sheer ecstasy. 'And do you really want to marry me?' she asked when she finally could.

'Of course, you silly little thing.' And Frances gave a sigh of sheer relief and leaned her frizzy head against his chest.

Harriet, returning home, blinked at the scene in her own hall. Jane was crying quietly and being held closely by the comte while her little maid had hysterics in a corner, and then her bemused eyes focused on her husband and she hurled herself into his arms.

'What have I come home to?' he said, gathering her in his arms. 'Here is the Comte de Mornay with tales of murder, treachery and mayhem, and Miss North, who says she is not Miss North but Lady Jane Fremney and that her father has found out her whereabouts.'

Still holding Jane close, the comte said over her head, 'Lady Jane will tell you every-thing, Duke, but I have some business with

218

the authorities which is pressing. Take care of her for me.' He bent his head and kissed Jane on the cheek.

Harriet, despite the fact that she did not want to leave her beloved husband's arms for one moment, moved to Jane's side and said quietly, 'Come with us. What happened? Do not cry. Is your father returned?'

As they moved up the stairs to the drawing room, Jane dried her eyes and tried to compose herself. In a flat voice she told them all that had happened to her at the Farleys'.

When they were seated in the drawing room, the duke said, 'He was probably nothing more than the paymaster for some inefficient organization of treacherous malcontents. De Mornay sounds like an efficient fellow. He will soon sort things out. All you have to do is try to recover from your shock.'

'Clarence Farley sent an express to my father telling him where I am,' said Jane, beginning to cry again. 'He will come and take me away.'

Harriet rapidly explained Jane's situation to her husband. 'Do not worry,' said the duke. 'We will give your father a hard time of it.'

'But I do not see what you can do,' wailed

Jane. 'I am not of age and he has every legal right to take me away.' The duke and duchess exchanged rueful looks over her bent head. 'Perhaps the comte will think of something,' said Harriet in a comforting voice.

But Jane would only shake her head. He had said he loved her, he had held her and comforted her, but she could not believe he would propose marriage. And how could anyone stand up to the tyrant who was her father?

For Jane the following week was a dismal affair. Still suffering from shock and expecting her father to arrive any moment, she stayed mostly in her rooms at Harriet's. The comte had called twice, each time to report to her how the traitors had been rounded up and the ringleader had proved to be a rich and eccentric City businessman who had bribed weak young men to join his cause. He had been arrested and taken to the Tower. There would be no need for Jane to give evidence, the comte would handle all that with his lawyers. They would take a statement from her to be read out.

And Jane's misery seemed to be intensified by the happiness about her. Frances, newly engaged, was floating on air, and Harriet and her husband walked about in a glow of rediscovered love.

One afternoon, as Jane was trying to listen to Frances's happy confidences, the butler entered and the words she had been dreading to hear fell on her ears.

'The Earl of Durbyshire.'

Frances gave a squeak of dismay and darted from the room, almost colliding on the stairs with a burly middle-aged man and a thin angular lady.

When the earl entered, Jane was standing by the fireplace. She felt all her luck had run out. If only Harriet and her husband had been at home to lend her a little support.

Behind the earl came the dreaded Miss Stamp.

'So you lied and cheated and tricked me,' roared the earl. 'It's bread and water for you when we get you back home.'

Jane tried to summon up some courage. 'I do not want to go with you,' she said. 'I am a guest here.'

'You are my daughter,' howled the earl, 'and you will do what you are told.' He seized her by the shoulders and shook her and shook her until the bone pins rattled out of her elaborate coiffure onto the floor and her hair cascaded about her shoulders.

'You are a wicked and evil child,' said Miss Stamp, who appeared to be enjoying herself immensely.

'Please leave my fiancée alone,' came a measured voice from the doorway.

The earl stopped shaking his daughter and swung round and stared wrathfully at the elegant figure of the comte. 'What are you talking about, you jackanapes!'

'Your daughter is to marry me,' said the comte, 'whether you wish it or not. Stand away from her.'

'I can do what I like with her. She's my daughter. What are you going to do about that, hey?'

The comte drew his dress-sword and looked thoughtfully at the naked blade. 'Kill you?' he suggested amiably.

There came the sound of feet thudding up the stairs and Frances tumbled into the room, followed by the hoteliers, Harriet, and the duke. She had been lucky in finding Harriet and her husband as they were returning home, and even more fortunate on her road to alert the hoteliers, finding them all approaching in an open carriage after making a call on one of their clients.

The Duke of Rowcester glared awfully through his quizzing-glass at the enraged earl. 'What are you doing in my home, and who are you?'

'I am Durbyshire,' said the earl. 'I am taking my daughter home and none of you is going to stop me.'

'I had just been explaining that Lady Jane is engaged to be married to me,' said the comte.

'Over my dead body,' shouted the earl.

'Exactly.' The comte looked him up and down with contempt.

'You do not have my permission to marry her and there's nothing you can do about it,' said the earl. 'Take her away, Miss Stamp, and get her to do her packing now.'

'I'm tired of all this,' said Sir Philip suddenly. 'It is all very easy, though why I should help a churl like you, de Mornay, is beyond me.' He scuttled up to Jane and took her hand and led her to the comte. 'Take her, de Mornay, and get out of here. Haven't you heard of Gretna? Take her away, man, and put that sword away. You don't want to murder this nasty man and hang for it. He ain't worth it.'

The comte looked down at Jane, at her hair tumbled about her shoulders, at her tear-stained face, and he sheathed his sword and swept her up in his arms. The hoteliers crowded around the fuming earl, defying him.

'And if you do anything or make a scene, I'll have all this in the newspapers,' said Sir Philip. 'You'll be exposed to London society as the bullying old fool you are. I suggest you thank your stars your daughter is marrying well and get out of here and take that long drip of acid with you.'

'I have never been...!' began Miss Stamp furiously.

'I can see that,' said Sir Philip, maliciously misunderstanding her. 'What man would want to get his leg over the likes of you?'

'Where is your room, my darling?' asked the comte outside the door.

'Upstairs, but...'

'We are not going anywhere, my love. I cannot take you off just like that. You need your clothes and belongings.' He began to carry her up the stairs.

Jane looked up at him dizzily.

'Are you really going to marry me?'

'Oh, my love.' He kissed her passionately and then said softly, 'As soon as possible. Which way?'

'Put me down,' said Jane, 'and I will show you.'

She pushed open the door leading to her

bedroom. 'Now we will stay here,' said the comte, 'until everything is quiet, and then perhaps next week we shall make a slow and comfortable journey north to Gretna.'

Jane looked at him shyly. 'I will have no dowry. And how did you ever find out my real identity?'

'I sent my efficient valet, Gerrard, into Durbyshire with a sketch of you to ferret out your secrets.'

'My father will never relent. I am penniless. I have nothing to give you.'

He wrapped his arms around her again and held her close. 'Oh, yes, you have,' he said softly. 'Kiss me!'

And Jane, brought up to be dutiful, did the very best she could.

NINE

To be in it [society] is merely a bore. But to be out of it simply a tragedy.

OSCAR WILDE

Three months had passed since the death of Clarence Farley, and the hoteliers sat in their private sitting room for the last time, each with their various thoughts.

Prince Hugo and his retinue had left, and below them the hotel was silent and empty of guests. Down in the kitchen Despard, once chef, now owner of the Poor Relation, which he had bought with all the money he had salted away, was entertaining Rossignole, his fellow chef, now partner, and a group of friends.

Sir Philip was moodily tapping out a tune with one hand on the piano. Lady Fortescue had had her way. They were all going to live together in a rented house in Manchester Square until such time when they found a suitable property, and only Lady Fortescue seemed happy with that arrangement.

Miss Tonks, who had wistfully dreamt of a home of her own and a husband of her own, thought drearily that they would all go on as usual until they died, even though they no longer had a hotel to run. Colonel Sandhurst had taken the arrangement to mean that Lady Fortescue did not want to marry him, and his life stretched out, dull and empty, to the grave. Mr Davy had been about to propose to Miss Tonks, but seeing with what seeming placidity she had accepted the new arrangement, he had come to the conclusion that she was happy for their friendship to continue, but nothing else. He was always conscious of the great difference between them in social status.

Sir Philip had not proposed to Miss Tonks either. There was no point. They would all be together just as before, and one of them would look after him in his rapidly declining years and he could not imagine why he felt so terribly old and depressed.

'I had a letter from Jane,' said Miss Tonks, breaking the moody silence. 'She says they were married at Gretna and are now staying with Scottish friends of Mr Ferguson outside Edinburgh. She thanks us all over and over again for saving her life. She is so much in love...' Miss Tonks fell mute again and silence came back, punctuated only by Sir Philip's playing the same phrase over and over again.

The door opened and Jack the footman and Lady Fortescue's old servants Betty and John came in, carrying bottles of champagne. 'A present from Despard,' said Jack, 'or Mr Despard, as I now must call him.' Jack looked very fine in a new coat of black superfine with black silk knee-breeches. He was to be the hotel manager, but Betty and John would follow their old mistress to Manchester Square.

'How kind,' said Lady Fortescue. 'Send Mr Despard our thanks and compliments, and do join us.'

'We are expected back at the party below-stairs,' said Jack. 'Do you wish us to stay and open the bottles for you?'

'I can do that,' said Mr Davy. 'Off you go.'

'Hark at him,' jeered Sir Philip, turning around on the piano stool. 'Gives the orders quite like the little gentleman that he ain't and never will be.'

Miss Tonks, correct to the last, waited until the servants had retired and said, 'Will you never have done with your nasty remarks, Sir Philip? The thought of putting up with your crotchiness from here to the grave depresses me beyond reason.'

'And the thought of looking at your stupid sheep face every day of the week is not much to look forward to either,' rejoined Sir Philip.

'Enough,' barked the colonel. 'Open a couple of bottles, Mr Davy, and pour us all a glass.'

Soon they were all sitting in a half-circle before the small fireplace, drinking champagne.

'A toast!' said Lady Fortescue, raising her glass. 'To our future together.'

'Future,' echoed several voices dismally.

She looked about her, her black eyes snapping. 'This is not a wake. We are rich, we are successful, and we are about to be back in society.'

Sir Philip, more affected by the champagne than the others, for he had been drinking earlier that day, said waspishly, 'You haven't got a heart.'

'I?' Lady Fortescue stared at him in amazement. 'I am all heart. I may say what I have done in keeping us together was out of thought for you all.'

'So here we are,' said Sir Philip, 'with the old colonel pining away there. Ah, yes, Colonel, I know your dream. You hoped for a place in the country with Lady Fortescue as your bride, a fine place with your horses and hounds, and she never even gave you a thought.'

'But I did,' protested Lady Fortescue. 'Did you not think that I would not rather be alone with my husband? But I could not leave Miss Tonks, or you, Sir Philip, to fend for yourselves.'

'Do you mean,' said the colonel, 'that you are going to marry me after all?'

'I did think that was the arrangement,' said Lady Fortescue.

'But Amelia, my heart, you said nothing to me of this.'

'I am saying it now. You and I will be married and...'

'You cannot want the rest of us around,' said Miss Tonks. 'I would not, were I married.'

'Well, nobody's going to marry you,' said Sir Philip spitefully.

'I know,' said Miss Tonks, and began to cry.

Sir Philip felt a pang of remorse. He was just about to propose to her when Mr Davy suddenly got down on one knee in front of Miss Tonks and drew her hands away from her face.

'Letitia,' he said in a low voice, 'I would

230

like to marry you, but I did not think I had hope because of the difference in our social situations, and because you seemed happy to live forever with the others.'

Amazement dried Miss Tonks's tears. 'But I want to marry you,' she shouted. 'I don't want to live with them.'

There was a stunned silence.

'More champagne, Colonel,' came Lady Fortescue's amused voice. The colonel re-filled the glasses. 'It looks as if I have caused a lot of unnecessary suffering. And now we have this house, but only rented. So I shall marry my dear colonel and Miss Tonks her Mr Davy, and we will all go our separate ways. But what of Sir Philip?'

'Oh, don't mind me,' said Sir Philip. 'I'm as happy as a lark. I'll leave you love-birds together and find more congenial company.' He stomped out, but, sad to say, the two couples left behind were too happy that evening to worry about him.

After chatting for ten minutes, Miss Tonks and Mr Davy rose and left the sitting room and made their way down to the hall and stood together under the light of the great chandelier. The doors, usually open to the fashionable crowd on Bond Street, were that night closed and barred. From downstairs, in the kitchen, came the faint sound of someone singing a song in French.

Mr Davy reached out and took Miss Tonks's hand in his own. 'Dear lady,' he said, 'it was a clumsy way to propose.'

Miss Tonks's thin face was radiant. 'Where shall we live?'

'I think I am a town creature. Would it trouble you to live in town?'

'Not at all,' said Miss Tonks dreamily, 'anywhere will do.'

'This place will always hold some exciting memories for you.'

Miss Tonks looked around, remembering how she had come here nearly destitute, frightened and lonely, to find companionship, warmth, adventure, and now marriage. 'It will always be dear to me,' she said. 'People who came here seemed to be always lucky in love. Jane was our last success, in a way, although we did nothing really to bring her and her comte together.'

Mr Davy kissed her gently on the lips. And then he said, 'I think, Letitia, you can count yourself as the Poor Relation's last romantic success.'

Lady Fortescue and the colonel, and Miss Tonks and Mr Davy were to have a double wedding, a *quiet* double wedding. But the end of Lady Fortescue's brave venture into trade amused the Prince Regent so much that he declared he wished to be present. Slowly the quiet wedding grew and grew, to become a fashionable affair. The Duke and Duchess of Rochester were to be there; the Marquess and Marchioness of Peterhouse, the marchioness being none other than their former colleague Miss Budley; then Lord Eston and Cassandra, who had worked for them at the hotel when she ran away from home; and Arabella and her husband, the Earl of Denby; and Captain Peter Manners and his little wife Frederica; and even Lord Bewley and his wife Mary. All the romantic successes of the Poor Relation were to be there. And then, just before the great day arrived, Jane and her comte turned up, declaring they would not miss the event for worlds. Society clamoured for invitations. It was decided to hold the wedding breakfast in the Poor Relation, now renamed The Grand, with Despard offering to supply the catering as his wedding present.

The Duke of Rowcester was the colonel's best man, and the Marquess of Peterhouse did the honours for Mr Davy, while his wife was bridesmaid to Miss Tonks, Miss Tonks's embittered sister having refused to even attend. Harriet was bridesmaid for Lady Fortescue. Miss Tonks was in white, as was Lady Fortescue – magnificent gowns of Brussels lace embroidered with gold thread and pearls, which had cost a fortune. Harriet was wearing that necklace, and Sir Philip could hardly bear to look at it. He had been through so much over that necklace and no one knew except perhaps that churl Davy, whose opinion did not count. The couples were married in the rented house in Manchester Square, which had been decorated with flowers for the occasion.

Lady Fortescue and her colonel were correct and dignified, as was to be expected, but the Marchioness of Peterhouse, the former Mrs Budley, declared that it was really Miss Tonks's day. Happiness had lent her a sort of beauty.

After the ceremony they all travelled to Bond Street and to the Poor Relation for the breakfast. The Prince Regent, who had failed to put in an appearance at the ceremony, arrived with his friends for the breakfast and kissed both brides, and the new Mrs Davy thought she might faint from an excess of exaltation.

'How wonderful it all is,' said Jane to her

comte. 'Everyone is so happy. I never thought when I first came here that such happiness would be the result.'

He laughed. 'Our happiness, you mean. I think the others have managed very well on their own. All I want to do is to take you away as soon as possible and kiss you senseless.'

Jane blushed, but her hand stole under the table and found his own.

Along the table from her sat Frances, drinking champagne and sparkling with happiness beside Mr Ferguson. 'It all ended well, don't you know,' said the irrepressible Frances. 'We will soon be married, and if I catch you even looking at middle-aged Scottish ladies, Jamie, I will scream!'

At the end of the breakfast, the Duke of Rowcester rose to toast the happy couples. 'The only sad thing about this day,' he said, 'is that it is the end of the Poor Relation as we all have known it, and there are many of us here who owe our happiness to the hoteliers.'

Sir Philip joined in the toasts. He was feeling increasingly miserable. They were all splitting up. The colonel and Lady Fortescue had found a pleasant house in Kent and would remove there on the following day, while Miss Tonks, now Mrs Davy, and her husband would take up residence in a handsome apartment in South Audley Street. He himself would stay on in the rented house in Manchester Square until the lease ran out in four months' time. The fact that his clothes were now of the best and that his jewels winked and glittered could not comfort his lonely old soul. He wished with all his heart that he himself had proposed to Miss Tonks. She had, as he now knew, lost hope that Mr Davy would ever propose to her, and so she would have accepted him, and he, Sir Philip, would not be facing a lonely old age.

When the first guests began to leave, he slipped away and walked outside into Bond Street. The sun was shining, intensifying his loneliness. He looked up at the hotel, at the sign 'The Grand,' and thought it a silly sort of unoriginal name. No more guests to worry about, no more frights, no more adventures, no more poverty. He felt like crying. He would go to Limmer's and get drunk. Tears filled his eyes and he turned away blindly and collided with a lady who was walking along with her maid. He whipped off his hat and stammered out his apologies.

'Sir Philip!' exclaimed the lady, a statuesque matron with large teeth and improbable blonde curls peeping from under her rakish bonnet. 'Do you not remember me? Susan Darkwood?'

He bowed low and then realized she was dressed from head to foot in black. 'Your husband...?'

'Lord Darkwood died six months ago.'

'I am so sorry. You and your husband were among our first guests.'

Lady Darkwood giggled. 'Did we not have fun then? And poor little Harriet came up from the kitchens to marry her duke. And now you are all so fashionable and little me was not even asked to the wedding. Still, it must be a happy day for you.'

'Not for me. I am alone again.'

She heaved a sigh. 'As am I. Ah, here is my carriage. You will come home with me and we will take tea and talk of old times,' said Lady Darkwood, who would not have dreamt of entertaining such a lowly creature as Sir Philip in the old days.

He hesitated. 'I am not very good company.'

She smiled down into his eyes. 'Then we must think of something to cheer you.'

His elderly heart suddenly began to thump against his ribs. He smiled back. 'I should like that. I *need* that. The company of a beautiful lady would do me a power of good.'

'Wicked man.' She tapped his hand with her glove. 'Come along.'

As happy as he had so recently been sad, Sir Philip climbed into her carriage and took the seat next to her. He pressed her hand and she gave him a languishing look.

The carriage moved on and rolled down Bond Street, away from the hotel.

And Sir Philip Sommerville did not look back.

Not once.

The publishers hope that this book has given you enjoyable reading. Large Print Books are especially designed to be as easy to see and hold as possible. If you wish a complete list of our books please ask at your local library or write directly to:

Magna Large Print Books
Magna House, Long Preston,
Skipton, North Yorkshire.
BD23 4ND

This Large Print Book, for people
who cannot read normal print,
is published under the auspices of

THE ULVERSCROFT FOUNDATION